Dissent in the Ranks

Mr. Darren says it's all about timing.

And lately it seems like my timing's always wrong.

Like when I am standing at my locker with Keenan right after language arts and he says, "So, did you see *Teen Supernova?*" He's talking about a reality show where teens compete to be the next version of this pop star called Avatron. The winner is usually lame, but some of the contestants are pretty great.

"Nah," I say, cramming my books away and getting out my lunch. "I recorded it. I was practicing and then playing *Liberation Force.*"

"Nice," says Keenan. "I meant to get online too, but Skye says we have to watch *Supernova* live now that it's the semi-finals."

"Well, don't tell me what happens," I say.

Then Skye shows up and does her usual thing, huffing and slouching against the locker beside Keenan's like she has no skeleton. "That. Was. A. Travesty," she says in that way she does when she disagrees with something, which is most things. And then before Keenan or I can even stop her, she goes off: "There is no way that Starleena Fox should have been purchase-voted off before Cassidy McClane!"

"Whoa!" I shout, and I hear Keenan sigh because he knows what I'm about to say and that I'm right. "Duh, no spoilers! I just said I didn't watch it yet!"

Skye narrows her eyes at me like she does, where one eyebrow rises up like a hissing cat and her mouth falls open in that annoying way where you can see the white gum that she is always chewing.

"Oh, excuse *me*, Anthony," she says. "It's not my job to keep track of your schedule every second of the day."

"You could use your brain for once!" I say back.

And when I say that, I know that Keenan is going to have to say something to defend Skye. The two of them have been dating for like three and a half weeks now, which is pretty much a record for our class. They're one more week away from going to their *second* dance together, and that's basically as boring as marriage. Pretty soon they'll be just like one of those couples down at Pacific Place with the matching black jackets who walk together all quiet—because what's left to say at that point in your life?—the same ones who always get annoyed when we talk during a movie and it's like, *duh*, if you want to see a movie in silence, rent it! But anyway, I get that I just insulted Keenan's girl and so he's obligated to step in.

"Hey!" he says, puffing out his chest. "Back off, Fat Class!"

Whoa. I can't believe those words just came out of his mouth. Keenan and I have been friends since forever and he's got all kinds of dirt on me and anything else would have been fine right then—but bringing up Fat Class? That's the one thing that should be off-limits. I notice a couple of our classmates' heads turning too, and all of it just makes me snap.

"Shut up!" I shout, and slam him into the lockers.

And right as Keenan's girly shoulders clang against the blue metal and everybody within ten feet goes "Ohhh!" who just so happens to be walking by?

Mr. Scher.

"*Anthony!*" he barks like an attack dog, and actually he looks like one too, with that stupid bald head and white beard and those too-white teeth, like he sits at home in his secret evil basement and polishes them before he heads out for his second job as a child-abducting vampire. "Office! Let's go. No, now."

"What? I didn't do anything!" I say. And it's so annoying because if it was any other teacher, especially a young one like Mr. Travis or Ms. Rosaz, it would be no big deal. They are both kind of scared of us eighth graders, especially kids like me and Keenan who look older. I am fourteen and Keenan will be too in January, and it's, like, come on! Most fourteen-year-olds are in high school already. A little friendly shoving between two friends shouldn't matter.

"I don't want to hear it," says Scher, motioning for me to follow him. "Come on."

"This is so unfair!" I say, but I fall in line behind him as he struts toward the office, because no matter what happens, I cannot get in big trouble these next two weeks.

The Only Mission That Matters

Fall Arts Night is in twelve days. And that's one of only two chances all year that me and Keenan get to rock out onstage in our band, the Rusty Soles. We're in Rock Band Club after school, and we're working on a song for the concert, and if I get in trouble and miss it, the next chance to play anything other than our friends' basements isn't until spring.

And that is forever from now.

Stalag Catharine Daly K-8

"We were just messing around!" I add as I trail behind Mr. Scher. "It was no big deal."

Well, except what Keenan said was kind of a big deal.

But Mr. Scher is never going to listen. He seems to take our size and age like personal challenges, like it's his mission to prove to us that we still belong here, that *he's* still in charge. "Life isn't fair," he says over his shoulder.

And even though I don't want to get in trouble, I can't

help muttering a string of curse words under my breath. I don't say it loud enough for Mr. Scher to hear the words, but he can tell I'm saying something and he whirls back around.

"Excuse me?" He glares at me. "Do you also need the automatic detention for not using school-appropriate language?"

I glare right back at him. "No."

School-Appropriate is one of like twenty terms and phrases that teachers are always reciting at us, like they were all brainwashed during their enemy training. Things like **Compassion Is Courageous, Excellence Takes Effort, Student Accountability.** But **School-Appropriate** is maybe the worst, and I get it all the time:

"Anthony, that language is not . . ."

"I know that's what someone might say if his arm was being eaten by a zombie, but your story needs to be . . ."

"The slogan on that T-shirt is not . . ."

It's so ridiculous. We hear swears in everything we watch and listen to: movies, video games, TV shows, music. And we have for years. Also, news flash: we *children* have been swearing among ourselves since we were like six.

Plus, these teachers are hypocrites. Have I heard them swear tons of times when they're talking to each other? Of course.

But whatever, it's just more of the same in this stupid stalag of a school.

If I lived in another part of town and went to one of the real middle schools that is only sixth, seventh, and eighth grades, I bet things like this incident with Mr. Scher would never even happen. But Catharine Daly is a K–8 school. I mean, sixth and seventh graders might as well be puppies with how dumb and babyish they are, but at least they've learned the basics, like how to avoid an eighth grader and how to put on deodorant. Have you smelled fifth graders? Heard fourth graders? Have you been slimed by anything under the age of nine? There are all these little kids everywhere all the time, and they're always sneezing or licking something or crapping their pants.

And because of them, we eighth graders are expected to **Lead by Example** at all times, and that's nearly impossible. Eighth graders are not made to set a good example. We are made to battle in the trenches between being a kid and being a teen. Setting a good example is also a good way to get your leg blown off by a land mine.

Trapped Beneath the Ice

Ms. Rosaz is always nagging us to use figurative language. So here you go, Ms. Rosaz, here is a simile to describe eighth grade:

Being in eighth grade here is basically like being stuck under the ice in a frozen pond, and you can see up through the glassy surface but you can't break out. There's a level like this in *Liberation Force 4.5: Axis Payback*, the multiplayer game that Keenan and I have been playing nonstop. It takes place during World War II, and you are crossing the ruined European countryside taking on the Nazis, which is so much cooler than trying to steal some stupid blue dragon's magic crystals or whatever.

In Level 18, you are by the Ourthe River at the start of the Battle of the Bulge, Germany's last big offensive in December 1944, and during a firefight you fall through the ice. You die there a few times trying to break through to the surface. Finally, you figure out that the ice is too thick, and that instead you can swim down and find a sewer tunnel. It leads you right into a Nazi bunker, where you die a few more times, but at least from there you can fight your way out.

There is no secret tunnel out of eighth grade.

I mean, I am sixteen months from driving a motor vehicle! On a road! With other lives in my hands! I can *see* high school up there above the ice. I would already *be* in high school if some stupid hippie preschool teacher named Birch didn't convince my parents that because I was behind in my motor skills and self-control, and because boys aren't as ready as girls or whatever, I would benefit from an extra year in preschool. So I was just sort of a big floppy spaz when I was four—who isn't?

But instead of being a freshman, I am stuck here going numb, pressed up against the ice as my oxygen meter slides from green to yellow to red, and following Mr. Scher to the office, where one little bit of bad timing suddenly has my musical future hanging in the balance.

In the Lair of the Kommandant

When we get to the office, Mr. Scher has to interrupt Principal Tiernan's daily flirting with the PTA dads, so she gives me that glare, the one she thinks is intimidating but really just makes her look ridiculous. She's so annoying: all old but she tries to look young, with the smooth dyed hair and the shimmery skirt-and-shirt outfits and the spiky cougar heels, her eyelashes like furry spiders. The dads love it, though. Even my dad gets all smiley when she tosses him that patented wink of hers.

"I'm going to have to call home about this," Ms. Tiernan says once Mr. Scher has laid out the details of my crimes. The call home is nothing new. That's going to suck, but it's what she says next that will determine my fate.

I watch her mull over the possible **Consequences of My Actions**. The makeup caked on her forehead buckles as she puts on her thinking face and taps her chin with her finger. Even this expression seems to be just in case there's a stray dad in the vicinity. Like she's so in control, so on top of everything.

"You can eat lunch here on the couch," she finally says, "then miss free period . . ."

None of that's a big deal. Almost there . . .

"And you can miss free period tomorrow too." She struts away, heels clacking.

Yes! I make an Allied "V for Victory" to myself and grab a seat on the black leather couch. Missing free period does stink, but whatever. Keenan and I probably need to cool off anyway.

As long as Tiernan didn't threaten to take away Rock Band Club or Arts Night, I can weather any punishment.

Time in Solitary

The couch isn't that terrible a place to be. You get to watch the daily parade of carnage: sick kids, hurt kids, kids who did crazy stunts and got caught. You hear Ms. Simmons, the secretary, calling home, see the stressed-out moms running in.

Some of today's cases are pure comedy, like when a fourth grader staggers in covered in his own snot with a plastic knife lodged in his nose that he was using to try to retrieve a corn kernel. They get the knife out but the kernel will never be recovered.

But then there are the soldiers of the resistance, keeping up the fight against all odds: like a sixth grader who got busted for forging his mom's signature to try to get out of taking the citywide standardized test. As he stands there, red-faced—Tiernan winking her way through one of her most sadistic tools of torture, the live call to your mom's work with you standing right there—our eyes meet and I give him a little nod. Keep fighting, young one. Someday, you'll be on the front lines, and this black couch will be yours.

I finish my lunch and things quiet down during free period, which only means that as a middle school student you are free to be bored in the library or the courtyard. You could go out to the playground, but that's where all the little kids are having recess.

Sitting there, I think back on that moment at the lockers. Even though Skye was wrong to just blurt out spoilers, I realize that maybe I've also been getting frustrated with her easily this year, ever since we dated last summer. It barely lasted two weeks and I'm over it. I totally am! I mean that was like three months ago, ancient history at this point, and everybody knows that nothing really works out in the summer anyway because you barely see each other except for online and texting. We only actually hung out twice, once at the mall and once at Magnuson Park, where we went swimming in Lake Washington. And then I guess I forgot to text her back a couple times right around when I got *Liberation Force* for my birthday, and then that was that.

We've smoothed it over, but now that she's dating Keenan, I have to see a lot of her. She's been looking really hot this year too. Like today she's wearing this cool sweater-vest-and-button-down outfit with pencil jeans. She has a pretty sweet body, but she doesn't flaunt it like some of the other girls in our class. Her hair is dyed kind of bloodred (the natural color is like a sandy blond, but Skye says she is *not* a blonde) and falls down the left side of her face. It's a look that says hotness but also some brains, like she spent five minutes on it but not ten. Skye doesn't want to be one of those cute-bots that seems to spend their entire existence trying to look exactly like my little sister's Polly Pockets. It's the difference between looking good and looking perfect and plastic.

And so, I guess sometimes, even though I'm not into her, I maybe still think that she's hot, or maybe miss dating her kinda . . . that is, unless she is going and opening her mouth and making me crazy.

But it's been fine, no big deal. And of course none of that is Keenan's fault. He definitely waited long enough before he started dating her. And it was Skye's idea, and Keenan asked me if it was okay.

Still . . . it's been a long three and a half weeks being around them being together.

Closing Ranks

The rest of the day is dumb: after free period, it's social studies and math, and I make sure to just keep my head down and go unnoticed.

I don't see Keenan and Skye until we're back at our lockers at dismissal. I wonder if either of them will still be mad, but it's business as usual. I can't help feeling in a better mood too. It's Thursday, which means Keenan and I have Rock Band practice.

"Still good for the show?" Keenan asks immediately.

"Yeah," I say. "Unless my parents freak out."

"She called home?" Keenan asks.

"She said she was going to. And when's the last time Tiernan forgot to torture a kid?"

"That's so ridiculous," says Skye as we walk to her locker, she and Keenan with their arms around each other, slouching their single Siamese body along beside me. "You guys are best friends! They should know you were just kidding around. It was so nothing important!"

"I know," I say.

"I think Scher *wants* to get you kicked out of Rock Band," Skye continues. "I bet he totally gets off on that idea."

It's nice to have allies again, but I wish Skye would just drop it. She's one of those girls who *always* have opinions. And not, like, after carefully considering anybody else's point of view—with Skye it's like ninja opinions that just drop down on you like *bam!* before you even have a chance to maybe work through some of the sides of the issue or anything. I've never seen her dwell. Or mull. (Yeah, I know those words, Ms. Rosaz, even though you don't think I do.)

Then again, I should probably be annoyed with me, because I didn't think her opinions were annoying before we broke up. What I used to think was that it was cool the way Skye could say what was on her mind so fast. I can't do that, except if I'm mad about something. A lot of times I feel like by the time I think of what I want to say, the moment is over.

Skye packs her bag, grabs her coat, and pulls out a large sign attached to a piece of wood.

"I bet Tiernan was just looking for an excuse to call your dad and hit on him," she says as we make our way to the front doors, and we all do laugh at that, though maybe me a little less. I'm not looking forward to dealing with the fallout at home.

"All right, well, later," says Skye. She slobbers a kiss on Keenan's cheek and I try not to look, because it's like Keenan is getting attacked by a jellyfish (except maybe I remember what those kisses felt like).

"Oh!" Skye rummages in her shoulder bag. "Here, take these, and could you wear them tomorrow? That would be great." She hands us each a button and then heads outside to meet up with her friends Katie and Meron.

The button says the same thing that the three girls start shouting among the stream of departing kids, and the same thing their signs say: WINKY NEEDS ACTION.

The button also has a hand-drawn sketch of Winky, the little injured sparrow that lives in the school courtyard. Ever since the bird flew into a window back in September and broke its wing, Skye has been on a mission to save it. Ms. Tiernan wanted to have it caught and removed, but Skye successfully protested that it would be cat food in the wild, so they should let it live there. She and her friends built it a birdhouse, and she feeds it each week.

Their latest crusade is to get a female sparrow to live with Winky, to improve his "quality of life." Meaning so he can make some baby sparrows. So they're trying to raise money to have someone from the Audubon Society bring a female bird in, along with netting to kind of force them to date. Their fund-raising is going slow, but typical Skye shows no signs of stopping. You kind of have to hand it to her, standing out there in the sea of kids leaving, shouting her lungs out to help a dumb bird.

And we'll get an earful if we don't wear the pins, so Keenan and I put them on before heading up the hallway.

Convicted Without a Trial

Now that it's just Keenan and me, I realize that our fight earlier is still on my mind. I feel like I don't want to turn too much in his direction.

"You have time to play *LF* tonight?" he asks.

"Depends on the stupid phone call," I say. Odds are my parents will be mad but not grounding-mad. Game time could be on the line, though, which sucks, and I am reminded that all this *sucks*! Like one little intense moment between friends even freakin' matters!

Well, but Fat Class mattered.

The comment. I mean, a little. But I know Keenan only said it in the heat of battle. He knows it's not really Fat Class, that calling it that is just a joke.

Except sometimes it maybe feels like Fat Class.

So the deal is, I'm overweight. Actually, if you just go by my body mass index, the All-Powerful BMI, I'm technically obese. By one stupid digit! Which is extra dumb because I don't look that fat and it's not like I'm busting out of my clothes or anything. I just wear baggy jeans and my hoodie and it's all good.

But the real problem is that on the inside I'm what's called prediabetic. It has to do with your blood sugar and other stuff and the point is, if I don't lower my weight and watch my diet I could end up with type 2 diabetes, which is the kind that onsets when you're older.

"There's still time," the doctor said at my last checkup, but he said it with this look in his eye like the bullets had hit vital organs and I was already a goner.

So that's why Mom signed me up for Fat Class. It's really called Life-in-STYLE! but even I'd rather call it Fat Class than *that*. It's one of those classes that are mainly for grown-ups and old people. I'm the only kid there. But actually, that's what makes it okay. Nobody at school sees me, and compared to the older guys I do okay at all the exercises.

I mean, I guess I wouldn't really care if my classmates knew I went. They all know I'm not some athletic type. It's just easier to give them as few bullets to use against you as possible.

Girls and Snipers

Which is why it hurts that Keenan would use that kind of ammunition. And I feel like he never would have done that before Skye. Keenan is my best friend and bandmate and we always used to know which things would be annoying and irritating to say just to push each other's buttons but also which things we shouldn't bring up.

It's not cool how a girl can screw all that up. Suddenly everything is freakin' life-or-death all the time. Like today, when what should have been just normal Keenan and Anthony joking at our lockers like old times ended up feeling like Level 13 of *Liberation Force*. Which is to say that girls basically make life feel like when you're trying to take out the bell tower sniper during the Battle of Metz in November 1944. The bridge is out because you missed a hidden land mine on the last level, and then suddenly your buddies are going down and you lose your medic and you have to run the blockade on foot to get that stupid sniper before you can start your assault on the final panzer, and there are bullets everywhere and dust and rubble and screams and pain.

I barely even see Keenan outside of school anymore except as a GI in the game. We used to have a good pattern of hanging out, like on Sundays when we'd get doughnuts and chais at Top Pot and then sneak them into the early matinee at Cinerama. Or when we'd get mochas and sit in the aisles at Secret Garden Books reading the graphic novels and showing each other the cool panels. It was like reading two books at once. But now all that time is gone.

I wonder if I should say something to him about all this now. But I'm not sure what. Not that it's a problem that he's dating Skye or anything, and he probably knows that he crossed the line with the Fat Class comment. Just, in the future, maybe . . .

But we're already up the stairs and Keenan is asking, "Did you practice the new tune?"

And I feel like it's too late.

Maybe it will come up another time. Or maybe I'm just a wimp. Whatever! Rock Band is our time and I'm not going to let some stupid moment that was probably Skye's fault get in the way of our friendship.

So I just answer his question. "Yeah. Worked on the song a lot, and also started learning some of *Arcane Sweater Vest* too."

That's the new album by the Zombie Janitors. It's sick. Those guys are hilarious too, for a metal band, which is obviously because they're British. They're our second-favorite band after SilentNoize, but the Noize hasn't put out an album in like two years because their lead singer, Jake Diamond, is at some kind of holistic mineral detox spa in Sedona and their old drummer left to start a ringtone-only record label.

"Yeah, I started working through the ZJ album too," says Keenan. "I didn't practice much for today, but I'll rock it."

I nod because Keenan will. He's a really good bass player. Almost as good as I am at guitar.

We pass the cafeteria and arrive at a door with a hand-painted sign that says Student Lounge. I can feel the floor vibrating already, and that hum in my sneaker soles makes the stupidness of this whole day finally seem to shake loose, like it's a crust that has cooled around me and now I am bursting free of it like some awakened mutant, raining down flakes of rock on the terrified scientists who discovered me.

Finally, it's time to rock.

Why Mr. Darren Rocks

"Mr. Cantrell, Mr. McCartney, welcome." Mr. Darren is sitting on a brown metal folding chair with his Les Paul across his lap. He's got it hooked into the Line 6 amplifier and has it set to a wicked crunch distortion. It sounds like a hive of hollow-tipped knives. (Ms. Rosaz, you never knew I could describe things like that, did you? That's because you just make us write stupid memoirs and five-paragraph essays instead of asking us to describe music.)

My last name obviously isn't Cantrell. It's Castillo. But Mr. Darren always anoints us with the names of killer rock musicians, based on who he thinks we've been sounding like, and so lately I've been Jerry Cantrell from Alice in Chains. Other times I've been Mr. White, Morello, Page, Slash, Perry, and so on. After a long day, it's nice to have someone treat you like who you *could* be, instead of what you *aren't*.

What's also cool is that Mr. Darren isn't just picking today's superstars—he's not calling me Trohman or Koenig, even though they are who lots of kids think of as the best guitarists. Some kids act like the guitar was invented last week, and like any music that's not on the sound track to the latest horror movie is irrelevant.

Paul McCartney is about the oldest reference that Mr. Darren uses, and yeah, he's older than my grandfather at this point, but we've spent some time putting our ears on the *Sgt. Pepper* bass lines and you kinda have to pay your respects to Sir Paul.

Mr. Darren is up on the second of three curved levels that are built into the floor. Before this place was a student lounge, it was the band room. Rows of kids used to pack in here and play flutes and stuff, but then the school's formal music programs got cut.

The only thing that changed during this room's brief life as the world's worst student lounge was that they added three couches and a soda machine. Except then a bunch of parents freaked out because soda is the **Worst Thing Ever**, and then people started writing obnoxious messages on the whiteboards, and finally a kid broke his ankle leaping from one couch to the other, and that was the end of that.

Rock Band Club was actually Ms. Tiernan's idea. She got a bunch of music gear donated to the school, probably using six thousand of her best winks, and then hired Mr. Darren, who was already around tutoring kids in math. The lounge was the only free space in the building, and so now the couches are pushed against the wall, and there are amps, drums, speakers, and guitar cases everywhere. You can still kind of read the echoes of the nasty messages on the boards, and there are still brown soda stains in the carpet, but otherwise, this room went from being the worst to the coolest place in school.

For everything that is unbearable about Tiernan and Catharine Daly, no other school in the city has a Rock Band program. When I'm actually safe inside this room, I can remember that.

Mr. Darren is chunking on the sixteenth-note riff that's part of the song we've been working on this fall, the one that we have less than two weeks to finish.

"How was the war?" This is how Mr. Darren always asks about our day.

"A few casualties, sir," I say, "but we took the hill."

"All right then," he says. "Let's fire it up."

Mr. Darren is cooler than any other adult in school by far. He is never stressing or making music feel like homework. And even though I see him talking to the other teachers, he never brings up things that have gone wrong in other parts of our day. When we get here, he's just about the music.

It's awesome too how he actually pays attention to what we're into, like using war lingo with us. Also, we've talked with him about how World War II was actually, like, a good war. Real heroes, real villains. Ever since then, war has basically sucked. It's this complicated thing that makes your parents get in fights with your uncles, and it seems like nothing with the far-off deserts and dictators and the oil and the villages is worth dying for. Case in point: tons of kids' parents wouldn't let them play *Liberation Force 3*, which took place in Afghanistan, and yet this version, set in World War II, is like the top-selling game ever.

Some other ways that Mr. Darren is cool: he actually cares about how he looks, unlike so many adults. He has a rock haircut, dyed black, and he wears jeans that are actually in style. And even though he's married and has two kids, he's still in two bands, called the Breakups and Subdivisions on Mars.

We've only seen him perform once. The Breakups played at school one time, which was pretty great except for the fact that it was at three in the afternoon and lots of parents came. A couple of them knew the Breakups and actually started dancing a little bit right there in the school gym, and, ooh, not good. Luckily, Keenan and I got to be roadies for the day, tuning guitars and running the sound system, so we were able to mostly ignore that display. And then Mr. Darren and his band were really good.

We've also watched videos on YouTube of his band from like fifteen years ago called Tender. There is young Mr. Darren, with spiked hair, playing in Europe and even on *Saturday Night Live*. That must have been sweet!

Still, I wonder if it's weird to be a has-been like that. I don't mean that in a bad way, like he's pathetic or anything. Just that he *has been* those things and now he's not. That's got to be strange. Sometimes, when Mr. Darren is talking about what his current bands are up to, he sounds a little flat, and

I wonder if he's thinking back to those awesome times with Tender and wondering how he ever ended up in some gross student lounge with a couple of teenagers.

And yet, when the topic is us and our music, he is always enthusiastic. He acts like what we're doing is just as important as any other part of our school day, maybe even more important, because music is about expression and connecting people. He makes it feel like a noble calling, not just a cheap *extracurricular* activity, and definitely not something you could just *take away* like we're children and it's a shiny toy. If more teachers were like Mr. Darren, school would suck so much less.

The One and Only Merle

"You two ready to work on the Killer G tune?" Mr. Darren asks. "It was sounding great last time. Definitely another memorable Rusty Soles hit."

By the way, our band name was Keenan's idea. And before you ask, yes, the spelling like feet is intentional. Like we're all robots, and since we're in rainy Seattle our feet get rusty on the bottoms. He did a great sketch for an album cover where a giant rusty robot foot is about to stomp you. But also the name has the cool double meaning about your soul getting worn out.

I don't actually love the name, but we spent forever trying

to think of one and everything we came up with had either already been done, sounded stupid, or had no album art that you could imagine, and so here we are. My one good idea was the Flak Jackets. It was so great! But Keenan didn't like it, and Sadie, our lead singer, thought it was too "boy."

Sometimes I still think of new band names and suggest them to Keenan, just in case one ends up being better. Like the other day I thought of Androids with Neckties. Keenan didn't like that either. But Rusty Soles is fine, I guess. At least for now.

"And," Mr. Darren adds, "the clock is ticking for Fall Arts Night."

"Twelve days," says Keenan.

"Don't worry," says Mr. Darren. "That's plenty of time in rock and roll. Maybe today we can find that elusive second part."

"Cool," I say, grabbing my guitar case from the corner where I stashed it before school.

"I should tell you guys, though," Mr. Darren adds, "the other bands are starting to sound good. Could be some real competition for you."

I know he's kidding, but it still gets my competitive juices flowing. There is one band for each grade—sixth, seventh, and eighth.

"Bring it on," I say.

I lay my case down on the floor. It's one of those tweed ones and it's beat up because I bought it used, so I covered it with cool stickers. I flip open the latches and inside there she is:

Merle.

An Epiphone SG, used. It looks like a real Gibson, but Gibsons cost too much and besides the Epiphone is close enough. For now. I'm totally going to get a real Gibson someday. Maybe in high school if I keep saving my allowance, which is no easy thing but I try.

Merle is dark sparkle blue. I wanted the classic crimson blood color but we couldn't find one for the right price, and that's okay too. Merle is dented and scratched, but my dad had Colin over at Trading Musician fix her up. He says the intonation is a little weird as you go up the neck and sometimes I notice it but not really.

"What's up, Merle?" Keenan says.

I hold Merle out and shake it and make a deep, rumbling sinister voice: "All hail Sataaaannn . . ." (Don't worry, it's just a running joke between me and Keenan about old-school metal bands and how funny they were. Nobody needs to contact child services and no, we won't be coming to bite the heads off your hamsters anytime soon.)

And I know that Merle is the kind of name for a guitar that makes you go, *Um, Merle?* but here's the thing, it wasn't my choice. The original owner of this guitar etched the name into the body. The letters curve right around the volume knob. Nobody knows who that guy was, and I guess I could paint over them, or I could just call it Merle, so that's what I do.

Plus when I showed it to Keenan, after he was like, "Merle?" he said, "That's so cool!"

Keenan usually thinks weird stuff is cool. He cares a little more about image than I do. He works on his shaggy mess of hair and shops for clothes at vintage places like Red Light. Today he's wearing a navy blue bowling shirt with the name SAL stitched into it. I usually try not to stand out as much.

Merle is my one exception. Otherwise, it's okay with me if the only place anyone notices me is onstage, preferably after I just melted their brains out their ears and they are like, *Who is that?* and I'm just nodding and playing like, *Yup*.

Mr. Darren has cables out for us. I plug Merle into the Marshall amp that we've been dialing in to a perfect watery crunch. Keenan's bass is going through the Ampeg. We make a triangle, me standing on the curved level above Mr. Darren and Keenan.

Mr. Darren hits a low E and then taps a couple different octaves so we can get in tune. He never lets us use a tuner pedal unless it's performance time, because he says you have to develop your ear. "You need to be able to hear E and A everywhere in the world," he said once. I think that idea is cool, like how music is in the environment and if you can hear it, that's like having a superpower or knowing a secret code.

I slip a clear blue pick from my pocket. It's engraved with the two intertwined snake S's of Sister's Secret, our favorite underage band in town. I got the pick at a Vera Project show last summer. Their guitar player, Ty, threw it into the crowd.

Ty and the rest of Sister's Secret are sophomores at Ballard High. Ty was in the eighth grade band when we were in sixth grade. His band back then was called Beeblebrox! They were kind of mathy, but now Sister's Secret just rocks. They play at Vera all the time, and also High Point Community Center, and Ground Zero over in Bellevue.

Keenan and I talk about having our own real band when we are in high school. We imagine playing those all-ages shows, but it doesn't stop there, because we get so big that we tour the country, and then after high school we move to New York and keep getting bigger. Sometimes it feels like it could totally happen. Other times it just sounds like a crazy dream. But we still talk about it all the time.

We finish tuning and look to Mr. Darren. He always plays along with us. "One, two, three . . . ," he counts, and we are *in*.

The Killer G riff is cool. It's mostly on the low E string, and it's all sixteenth notes with lots of upbeats. It sounds complicated by itself, but once you lay it over a half-time drumbeat it turns into this giant iron tank rolling over the battlefield.

The three of us are sloppy at first, but Mr. Darren doesn't stop us or tell us we're doing it wrong because he knows you have to warm up, and so we keep looping it. It's an eight-bar pattern, and after a couple minutes we start to lock in. Our forearms spike up and down in unison, almost like bows in a symphony. Time starts to become bars, and soon the rest of the world is gone and music is all there is.

Until the door opens and Valerie walks in.

"All right, Ms. White is here," says Mr. Darren.

"Hey, Mr. Darren," says Valerie. She's our drummer, new this year after our drummer from the past two years, Liam, moved to Tacoma. Nobody at school had any idea that Valerie even played drums and we were worried because she doesn't really look the part, but then she came to auditions and rocked it.

"Hey, Valerie," I say, trying to sound cool, casual.

"Hey," she says, smiling for a half second before she looks away.

As she crosses the room I can feel Keenan watching me. He wants to see if I can keep my cool.

Because lately, around Valerie, I've been having a harder and harder time.

Girls Who Slam Drum Fills

The thing is, if you were sitting in my eighth grade class and you were checking out the girls for hotness, you wouldn't notice Valerie Clark because at first there is nothing to notice. She doesn't do all that stuff the Pockets do that makes them sparkly eye magnets. She's also kinda tall and big, but not *big* big, maybe just more like normal-sized, and she doesn't wear the really stylish leggings and low-cut shirts and all that the Pockets wear. And don't get me wrong, those outfits are hot, but it's not worth looking at for too long because the Pockets are only interested in a certain model of boy and Keenan and I have already figured out that we are *not* that type.

With Valerie it's weird because you're not sure what she's supposed to be. It's like she doesn't fit an obvious type. She never really dresses up: just wears jeans and either a flannel shirt or a hoodie every day, her dark hair back in a ponytail or braids. She has light brown skin and is maybe part Native American? I feel like maybe that's what she did her social studies presentation on last year, but I wasn't really paying attention. But the main thing about her look is that she doesn't seem to be that worried about it.

Keenan and I have been trying to decide if she's cute and I'm pretty sure I think she is, except I'm not totally sure because it's like her cute is written in another language. She's like when you're flipping channels and you stumble on a movie with the overdubbed Spanish and even though you know the movie by heart it feels different, and you can't be quite sure that it's the same because you didn't pay very good attention in Spanish class.

But then the drum playing starts.

Valerie walks up to the top level of the room and sits behind the five-piece cherry-red DW drum set. "Check it out," she says as she redoes her ponytail. She gets her sticks out of her stick bag, Vater 5Bs with wood tips, and then smacks down the opening fill to "D'yer Mak'er" by Led Zeppelin, ending it with a vicious cymbal crash. She and Mr. Darren have been going through the Zeppelin catalog and working out all of Bonham's sick drum fills.

"Nice," says Mr. Darren with a big grin. Sometimes he is just like any other guy with how a tight drum fill makes him completely happy.

"Thanks," says Valerie. She makes that half smile that she

has, the one that's not extra wide and fake like so many girls. It seems honest. You feel like you believe it.

"Yeah, cool," I say to Valerie, glancing at her for a nano-second. Her smile widens, and that makes me look away fast.

She warms up some more, now playing the beginning of "Good Times Bad Times." As she plays one of the rare cool cowbell parts in the universe, Keenan and I join in on the hits, and then Valerie rocks the tom fill and drops into the verse beat, you know the one, with the supercool triplet bass drum parts that she's *almost* got right. Mr. Darren jumps in and together we play the lead, him nailing it, me almost there, and Keenan plays John Paul Jones's completely under-rated bass line.

While this is happening I find myself watching Valerie, playing with her eyes closed, face scrunched in concentration, arms and legs in the flow, and out of the corner of my eye I feel Keenan giving me a look like, *Ha ha!* I want to glare at him but I just put my head down and focus on the music instead.

Because he's right. When Valerie plays you imagine things, like after rocking out at band practice you could grab burgers at Red Mill and then go to the movies together. And you could see something actually good with a girl like Valerie, something with guns and knives and guts but also with characters that aren't just clichés and definitely even something futuristic too. Or you could meet up on, like, a Saturday afternoon in Capitol Hill and watch the kids skate at Cal Anderson, and get slices at Big Mario's and then head over to Everyday Music and flip through the vinyl and make fun of the covers from the eighties.

I deserve the smirk from Keenan.

After Skye, I spent two months swearing off girls. I would never like someone again. But now . . .

Keenan keeps nagging me to ask Valerie out, but I have no idea how to do that. Or more like no idea what she would say. So I tell him to shut up and that I'm working on it. Soon. Maybe.

The Trouble with Singers

After another minute, our Zeppelin groove falls apart. "Okay," Mr. Darren says, "now we just need Sadie." His face twists in concern as he checks the time on his phone. "Any idea where she might be?"

"No clue," Keenan says.

"I know she's here today," says Valerie.

Sadie is our lead singer. She's actually in seventh grade, and also sings for their band. She is pretty great, but now that she's in two bands, sometimes she thinks she's a diva more than she should.

To tell you the truth, I kinda wanted to try out for singer. There were no eighth graders who wanted to audition, and when I'm at home in my room just recording junk, I work on writing lyrics, and it's kinda awesome. It's a different feeling to sing a song. To have it come out of you. Also it would be cool to be singing onstage and still rock the tricky guitar part.

Mr. Darren probably would have let me try out if I'd asked him. But I just didn't feel quite . . . ready. Besides, I don't exactly look the lead singer part.

And also, it could be weird, taking on two major roles in the band. I'm not sure how Keenan would feel about that. That's the kind of thing that usually leads to bands breaking up. That and girls. And everybody knows it's way better to be in a band. Solo artists always seem kinda lame and full of themselves, while bands always look really cool standing together like a team, a secret society, a band of brothers.

And Sadie is fine, except for thinking she's the best. Plus, she's missed a bunch of rehearsals because she's always getting detention for pulling crazy stunts or not doing her work. I guess that goes along with the whole lead singer personality, and also with being a seventh grader and not really knowing how to be cool yet.

"Well, we can start without her," Mr. Darren says, but then the door bursts opens and Sadie storms in like she always does. And even though it's probably the same old drama with Sadie, you can't totally ignore her because like any good pop star whose life gets told in embarrassing pictures online and in headlines in grocery store checkout lines, there is something about Sadie that makes you end up watching anyway.

Today she's wearing the skinny jeans and a black hoodie with big sparkly angel wings on the back. She has blond hair with red streaks, but it's messier than the usual Pocket look.

She slams the door and sighs heavily, like it's the world's biggest burden to have made it here at all today. So basically the usual. She heads straight for the couches and throws down her shoulder bag and then herself.

"Howdy, Ms. Harry," says Mr. Darren.

Sadie just huffs like that's such a stupid nickname, and sure it's harder to find as many cool female singers in rock but still that huff makes Mr. Darren's face fall just a little bit, and I hate seeing that. Nobody should give Mr. Darren any crap.

"We were just about to run Killer G," he says. "Did you want to sing your melody over it or try out any new lyrics?"

"Nah." Sadie is pulling like thirty things out of her bag, and then she picks up a glittery purple journal and a lime-green gel pen. "I've got some words that are almost ready, so I'll just work on them for a bit while you guys warm up." She says it like she's expecting a roadie to bring her a warm towel and some mineral water and a salad of weird greens while she does this.

I look at Keenan and roll my eyes. Sadie doesn't fool anyone. We all know she hasn't worked on the lyrics like she was supposed to and I want to yell at her like, come *on*, if everybody else in the band is trying to get it right then you need to try too! The show is so soon and you haven't even sung anything for the song yet!

But it was like this last spring too, and Sadie was totally writing lyrics right before we went onstage and then actually . . . she kinda pulled it off. Keenan and Liam and I had to agree that she sounded pretty great. But now Sadie knows she can pull it off at the buzzer, and the problem with that is: not every buzzer-beater shot goes in.

The Hidden Door in the Catacombs

"Okay," says Mr. Darren. He spins back to us. "Let's just run Killer G a bit and see how it goes. Valerie, count it off?"

"Sure." Valerie closes her eyes for a second and knits her brow. She's finding the tempo in her head like Mr. Darren tells us to do. Then she looks up and counts while clicking her sticks. She counts quiet compared to Mr. Darren, "One, two, three . . . ," then she slams four on the snare and we are in.

Sound overwhelms everything. We hear all the time these days that "loud" is bad and my mom would be all over me for not wearing my earplugs right now but she doesn't get how volume *feels* when it's all around you and you're in it and you're making it. The kick and snare attack like howitzers beneath the tinny machine-gun spray of eighth notes on the half-open hi-hat. Our chunky riff locks into the spaces in between and it is all our thoughts and I start to nod hard to the quarter notes. It's sounding good. Mr. Darren is grinning.

We loop the part, over and over. It's the best feeling ever, to just be playing, to just be in the music that is going from your brain to the muscles in your arm to the tiny pick to the tense string into the pickup, down the cord, and back at you from the amp and into your brain, only more powerful now with the extra boost of your bandmates. It's like you are building something that is getting bigger and more complete and, like, solid. Maybe it's some kind of futuristic tower like you see in pictures of Singapore or Dubai. The whole day is gone and you are just in the music, which is the exact *now*, and there's no more time or what happened before or whatever you have to do later or anything except the playing and the sound and it's the best!

With each pass-through, the riff gets tighter, gaps and joints melt closed, the tower rising. . . .

But then something strange happens, something that I'm not really expecting and I don't know if it's ever happened before. It's like my brain knows the Killer G part so well that I am rising out of it, out of the flow of the music, so that I am floating over it. Suddenly I am thinking back on my day, about the Fat Class comment, Mr. Scher and the phone call home, even Keenan and Skye, the duo that doesn't include me, and suddenly, even though I'm here playing music and so everything should be great, I'm getting really frustrated again.

It's like the energy of the music is connecting to my emotions, and saying, *Aren't you mad? Don't you want to change things?* And I do. I wish I could change everything that sucks.

And I'm even getting mad about being mad, because I am no longer enjoying this thing that is the best part of my day. That's not fair! I want to be back in the flow of the song with Keenan and Valerie and Mr. Darren, but I'm not, I'm floating over it like a ghost stuck outside the world of the living. Except I'm still hearing the tune . . .

Wait. No. Actually, I'm hearing something different. My ear doesn't *want* to hear this part anymore. It wants to be somewhere else. Like, it wants to go in a different direction. And I am hearing some*where* else we could go. It's kinda like in Level 14 of *Liberation Force* when you are running through the winery catacombs at Strasbourg trying to save the hidden French family and, after you've totally gotten bled out by the Nazis like ten times and you are so angry you want to smash your controller against the wall, you finally notice the door that's hidden in one of the alcoves. You bust through it and *that's* where the cache of fresh ammo and grenades is hidden, the one that you will need to win the level—

Outside my head the song crumbles to a halt.

"Anthony?" Mr. Darren says.

I look up and everybody has stopped playing. I realize now that I totally lost the groove and things got sloppy and fell apart. "Sorry," I say. My heart is pounding. "I . . . think I hear another part."

"Really," says Mr. Darren. "Do tell."

"Um . . ." I start sliding my fingers up the neck, tapping notes, and my fingers are twitching with nerves. I try to find the note I'm hearing, try to make the guitar match that tone. I press the E string down at A . . . close, is that it? Maybe not . . . up a fret to A-sharp . . . no, too far, back to A. Yeah, that's what I was hearing, or close enough. I stretch my index finger over the strings and clamp down, making the A major bar chord. The strings bite against my skin. I strum the chord. It sounds right. I start chunking eighth notes. "What if we went to here?"

"Ooh," says Mr. Darren. "Yes. It could go to A."

And now it's like I've shot off down this new shadowy catacomb with the straps of fresh grenades crisscrossing my chest and I can hear the mumblings of the hidden French family somewhere ahead and I'm not done yet.

"And then . . ." I play the A for two bars, then drop down and hit a D chord for a bar, then slide to E for the last bar . . . and back to A. Relief spreads through me as I return home because A feels like home now. I start the progression over. "How about that?"

Mr. Darren nods like he is impressed. "Let's try it," he says. "Valerie, maybe try moving your hi-hat pattern to the floor tom for this part and mixing up the kick and snare a bit. Let's do the G riff twice, then go into Anthony's new part."

Valerie counts off and we are back in, only now it feels like, instead of just going in circles, we are headed somewhere. Like we are standing on one of those moving walkways at the airport, heading toward the next part. It's scary because I don't know if it will work and I really want it to work and here it comes and we get to the end of the bar and now we all slide up to A . . .

And it feels great! It completely works! It's like we were meant to go there and *bam!* we blow the back wall of the wine cellar and escape with the French family out into the shallow gully, away from the Nazis. And then the teenage daughter with her fine video game physique is so grateful, and she says all this stuff in French and wraps her arms around you and gives you this big kiss and then it's on to the next level only this is even better!

"That's awesome!" Mr. Darren calls over the sound. He stops us and we tweak the progression, spicing up the rhythm a bit with a few syncopated upbeats.

While we're stopped, Valerie says, "Nice, Anthony." She is grinning, air-drumming the tom beat as Mr. Darren demonstrates a rhythm to Keenan.

"Thanks," I say, smiling back.

That feels good too.

We start up again with the changes and now things really are sounding good and I am so psyched because that was songwriting and that was *me*! The same Anthony that Scher and Tiernan only see as a black-couch resident, and we are going to play this at Arts Night, this second part that I found, and the song will be great!

"Okay, Sadie, hop on in here!" Mr. Darren calls over the groove, and he sounds so excited and the sound is so good that even Sadie can't resist.

She drags herself off the couch and walks up to a silver mic on a straight chrome stand. She adjusts the stand like a pro, strikes a pose with her hip cocked, and holds her journal out to read. We stop, then Valerie counts us back in to Killer G. Sadie mumble-sings, because of course she still doesn't really have lyrics, but her pitch is pretty good and her melody is catchy and we suddenly sound like a complete band.

Ladies and gentlemen, the stadium announcer booms, *the Rusty Soles!!!*

The crowd roars.

"Here comes Anthony's part!" Mr. Darren calls over the sound, and he nods and Valerie does a cool fill down the toms and *bam!* we change to the new part like doing a backflip into a pool. It takes Sadie a second to find some notes but she has good instincts and she goes up to a higher register than she was in for the first part, and so it's even bigger and we are totally going to nail this show, nail it nail it nail it—

Crashing Halt

But then the lounge door bursts open again, slicing my happy thoughts in half like strafing machine-gun fire. We grind to a halt in that car-crash way that happens when you stop playing abruptly.

It's Ms. Tiernan, and . . . uh-oh. I've never quite seen this look before. She's pissed. Like, for real. And looking right at:

Sadie.

"I'm sorry, Mr. Darren," says Ms. Tiernan. "I'm afraid I'm going to need Sadie to come with me."

Sadie's face has fallen and gotten red in a very un-Sadie-like way. Usually, she'd be freaking out and protesting about getting in trouble, but this time she doesn't even hesitate, just grabs her bag and follows Ms. Tiernan out. As she leaves she even mumbles "Bye," another thing Sadie would normally never do.

Uh-oh. I look at Keenan, and we know: whatever Sadie did, she's in real trouble, and that means so is the show.

Reality Drizzles

Sadie doesn't come back to practice. Another bad sign. We spend the rest of the time running the riff and the new part. By the end it's sounding really tight, but we are all quiet, worried about what's happened to Sadie, and to our band.

The school is empty when we're done at five. Valerie gets picked up by her older sister and Keenan and I walk home. It is misting out, and the kind of raw cold that for some reason feels colder than real cold. Keenan is wearing his black rain-coat and I am freezing in my charcoal hoodie and thinking back to this morning when Mom was like, "Take your coat," and I was like, "I don't need it," and now I'm annoyed that she was right.

Keenan and I are silent as we leave school grounds, lug-ging our guitars. Some of my thoughts have gone back to the fight earlier today, and the others are on Sadie, and it all adds up to a mood even darker than these rain clouds.

"What do you think was up with Sadie?" Keenan fi-nally asks.

"I don't know, but you know it's bad."

"Yeah."

We get to the intersection where our paths split and Keenan says, "Oh crap, you've got the whole thing with the call home."

"Ugh." With everything else, I'd completely forgotten about that. "Yeah," I mutter.

"Good luck," says Keenan.

Back to the Barracks

I walk another two blocks home. Our house is like the others on the street and in most of Seattle—a little craftsman. The only thing that makes it stand out is that it's this puke-yellow color that was supposed to be sunflower but came out too dark. My parents want to get it redone but they can't afford it right now and so we all kind of hate it together.

Also last year Mom and Dad had the whole front yard covered in gravel because if you water the grass these days you're personally responsible for killing the Earth. I remember eating lunch on that grass, and lying out there drawing. Now it's all shrubs and a little spiral stone path and a bench that nobody ever sits on. The backyard is a little better but it's mostly deck. That's how everything kind of goes in our house. Organized, structured, neat, except my room and I never hear the end of it about that.

Mom's car is in the driveway. She's been home a lot lately

because after she worked my whole life at Microsoft, some-thing to do with organizing people, they let her go. It was so cool when she worked there because she had the inside track on the best new games and stuff. I don't know what this Christmas will be like without that. Now she's got this idea to try to start some kind of environmentally friendly dry-cleaning business but it's expensive and these days nobody bothers to dry-clean things much and so that idea is kind of on hold and she is "regrouping."

And that means she's home. A lot. So those hours be-fore six, when I used to get home and grab some Doritos and Coke and play video games and then crank Merle up to floor-vibrating volume and let it out? Gone. The guitar playing has to be at a **Reasonable Volume**. The games have to be home-work. And the Doritos and Coke are long gone too.

And that also means there will be no delaying any fallout from a phone call home.

Daily Rations

"Hey, Ant," Mom says as I shuffle inside. I tense up. Here we go . . . but she shortened my name like she used to when I was little. That's a good sign.

So I reply, "Hey, Rosalie." This is one of the jokes I would make any other day and so I still make it, calling her by her first name in a tone kind of like we are pals or something.

"Don't be obnoxious," she says. "Here."

I drop my bag and toss my jacket and turn to find Mom holding out a plate of prison food. "What'll it be today, Mein Herr?" Another of my usual jokes.

"Anthony," she says, and she sounds edgy, but again, pretty much like any other day. She's always kind of crabby by the time I get home because she's been here all day and there's only so much "regrouping" you can do before everything is grouped and the house is so clean there might as well be velvet ropes and security guards everywhere.

I look over the plate. Let's see, Stalag VII-A, Allied POW 4356, what's on today's menu? We have five whole-wheat and flaxseed crackers, each covered in fat-free cheese spread, and three celery sticks, each with a spit-sized blob of almond butter. When you are prediabetic you have to know about how to eat to have good blood chemistry. The crackers have a lower glycemic index because they have more fiber, so it's like putting really inefficient fuel in your body that your system has to work harder to use, and that keeps you full longer. White carbs and sugar are like dry kindling, and whole wheat is like burning wet wood. The cheese spread has a lot of protein, and the fats in the almond butter are the good fats, and the celery is celery. I get why it's all good for me and why I need it. That doesn't mean I don't want to throw the plate against the wall and go back to my cell where I am secretly digging my tunnel out of here. Over on the counter is a glass of vegetable juice. Mmm, just like Coke.

But I just say thanks and take the plate and the glass. It

totally sucks to have already lost your Doritos and Coke privileges by age fourteen, but at least my parents and my sister, Erica, are eating this way too. Erica is no beanpole, and Rosalie definitely fills out her clothes. Dad is mostly thin except in spots.

I guess if I'm really honest I get that when it comes to food, we Castillos are in a stalag together, and the Germans are our genes, standing guard with uniforms and guns, while behind them the SS officers are the sinister scientists from the food corporations, cloaked in dark trench coats, planning new devices of blood sugar torture. They've already taken three of my grandparents, and an uncle on each side, to the chambers where they apply the triglycerides and the trans fats and the empty carbs until the blood glucose is through the roof and causing the heart attacks and the limb amputations. These stupid crackers and celery sticks are our Resistance, our tunnel out together.

Riot in the Cell Block

"I'll be upstairs," I say, and I am just starting to turn away when I hear the sigh from Mom.

"Principal Tiernan called."

Crap. Here we go.

I try to head off the attack. "Mom, it was so stupid. . . ." I can already see that tired look in her eyes, and even though

45

I know I am going to argue this one out, I still feel bad about doing it. I know I'm one of the things that make her so tired, even though that's not ever what I'm trying to do.

"It was just me and Keenan doing our thing," I add, "and Mr. Scher totally butted in and—"

Mom cuts me off. "Anthony, this is the third call home we've gotten this year already," she says. "It doesn't matter that you and Keenan are friends. You are in school, and there are rules, and you need to follow them and behave appropriately."

"Yeah, but the rules are for babies!" I say, and my voice rises but I can't help it because they are! "We were just blowing off steam and if we were in high school it would be no big deal!"

"You might feel that way," Mom says, "but you are still in eighth grade." Her voice is starting to rise too, and when she gets frustrated I know she'll make the leap, where one bad thing is suddenly also related to another bad thing.

"And what about your grades?" she asks.

There! The leap! Just like that!

"Who cares about my stupid grades?" I am shouting now.

"Are we going to see another report card full of Cs?" she says.

"I don't know! And why do you always have to make it about grades and never care about the things I'm actually good at?"

She looks more angry and more tired all at once. "Anthony, that is not what I'm doing."

"You didn't even ask me about band practice today!" I say. "You just went right to the stupid grades!"

46

And in another amazing stroke of bad timing, right then the door opens. Dad's home early from work. He has that tired look too, his tie loose and his gray suit rumpled from the car ride home. He works at a Chase bank downtown. I think he likes the routine of going to his job every day but I'm not sure how much he likes the job itself. Or maybe the reason he always looks beaten down when he gets home is that he does like his job and coming home to us is a drag, especially when he walks in the door to me and Mom going at it.

Of course he already knows about the phone call, and he probably heard the argument from outside, and so as he walks in he opens fire before his shoulder bag even hits the floor. "You better start caring about your grades," he says, like he's talking around a cigar stub, and then he just pulls out a grenade and lays waste to everything. "Or you're going to have to start missing out on your other activities."

There it is.

My only other activity is Rock Band.

"I didn't . . . ," I start, but I have no intention of finishing that sentence. I just want to make some protest sounds and get out before this goes any further. Actually what I want to do is scream at these adults—my parents, Tiernan, Scher, all of them—wielding their power over me like I don't even get a say. But I can't let this get out of hand, not with Rock Band on the line. Twelve days. Just have to make it twelve more days. "Fine," I mutter, and start upstairs.

"Anthony, are you hearing this?" Mom says.

"Yes! Where do you think I'm going right now? To do my

homework so I can be the valedictorian of your dreams!" I keep walking up the steps, cursing under my breath and adding so they can hear, "So stupid!"

"Anthony!" Dad snaps.

I stop on the stairs and sigh. "What?"

He pauses and takes a deep breath. When he speaks again, he sounds more calm. "How was practice today?" he asks. Dad used to play guitar so I think he likes that I do that too.

"It was fine," I say, and even though I sound annoyed, I'm glad that he is asking about music. It reminds me that on some level they care.

"Are you guys ready for the show?" Dad asks.

"Getting there." I don't mention the stuff with Sadie, but I decide to say something else and for some reason I get a little nervous feeling as I do. "I wrote a new part today," I say, turning half-around on the stairs, "to the song we're working on."

"Really?" Dad's face changes, like a puppeteer just brought him to life. He showed me his tapes one time, of his college band. He sang some of the songs. They were one of those weird jam bands from back in the nineties, but they were pretty good players. "I bet that was exciting," he adds.

"Yeah," I say, and it feels good that he thinks that. For a second I think about apologizing for the phone call home, because you can always tell when the right moment for that kind of thing is, and also I have this tight feeling inside. I don't want us to be mad at each other. I want them to be proud of me. . . .

But then I remember that the reason for the call was so dumb. Though maybe it would be good to just say it anyway . . . except now I am just standing there going back and forth like I always do, the right words never getting out, and then the moment feels like it passed.

"Maybe," Dad says, and he's talking carefully, like I'm a dangerous animal and he's the zookeeper, "you can get some homework done before dinner, and then after that you'll have time to practice a little for the big show."

This, I know, is a good time to just say, "Okay." To not exhaust them any further. To go upstairs and eat my rations and move on. It might be nice, someday, if I could actually make them proud. And Dad's questions remind me that Arts Night is actually a chance to do that . . . if Sadie hasn't ruined it.

Relief

I do spend some time on homework, and then we eat dinner, veggie burritos and spinach salad, stalag food that no one seems quite happy about, and then a dessert from the South Beach Diet that is custard and strawberries and a single dark chocolate square.

After dinner, I set up to practice our song. I run a red cord from Merle to a tiny blue Danelectro HoneyTone mini amp. It's only as big as your hand, so obviously it's not going to give you any kind of giant sound that you can feel, but it does make a nice little crunchy rock tone. I plug headphones into the amp, and then finally it's me and Merle again.

Time becomes the sections of the song. The universe becomes segments of four and eight, looping, repeating, but not just repeating, because each time you go through the part you play it better and hear more nuance and so you go somewhere deeper, and you feel all these new connections between things and feel how they fit.

I play and play, working on Killer G and the new part, which I've started calling Flying Aces. And that leads into other song ideas, and the rest of the day falls away, and when I finally look up the whole night has passed, my fingers and arms are sore, and I crash into bed with barely any thought.

Night Raid

Until my phone buzzes me back awake. Keenan. Probably pulling an insomniac *LF* session like he does—

Except his text says: *Did you hear about Sadie?*

I reply: *Hear what?*

But I feel like I already know before Keenan texts back:

Skye says she got suspended. Two weeks.

He texts again, but he doesn't need to. I'm thinking the same thing:

We're screwed for the show.

11 DAYS

The Crime

I wake up late, which makes my dad late and we're both silent in the car. I eat a banana and a cereal bar and he drives too fast, and then I rush to class. I trudge through the morning and don't have a chance to talk to Keenan until we're back at our lockers before lunch.

He just looks at me. "Suspended."

I feel the energy drain out of me again. "Do we know what for?" Even just speaking feels like the biggest effort ever.

Skye shows up and throws herself into a slouch against the lockers. "I got the dirt," she says breathlessly. "Sadie and Parker were in Ms. Rosaz's room for free period because they got caught cheating on the vocab test. And when the bell rang she left to make copies, but she'd confiscated Blake's phone earlier in the day and it was still on her desk. Parker knew his password, since they just broke up, so she grabbed it and they sent these nasty texts to a bunch of his contacts. But they sent one to his cousin by mistake, who told Blake's mom, and she called Rosaz."

"No way!" says Keenan, and he sounds kind of impressed because really that is some kind of combination of craziness and bravery even for Sadie.

"But how'd they get caught?" I ask.

Skye rolls her eyes and smacks down on her gum. "Because Mr. Scher saw them running out of the room, and they were laughing and stuff, and so he got suspicious."

"Of course," I groan. "It's like Scher's dream come true."

"And then Ms. Rosaz got the call," Skye says, "and she and Scher put two and two together and then tracked down Parker at the end of school and she confessed to Tiernan during interrogation."

"That's so stupid!" I shout, and I kick my locker shut in frustration.

"Anthony . . . ," says a serious voice, and I turn around and can't believe that *again* someone is walking right by at the worst time. At least this time it's Mr. Travis. He's new this year and apparently just got his teaching degree in Hawaii. He wears sandals even when it's raining and freezing and is always trying to have this mellow, cool vibe. He has a picture up in his classroom of him surfing. I think he means it to say, like, *Check it out, I'm a real person too!* but it is so not cool to have to see your teacher in a bathing suit. "Settle down, please," he says.

I resist the urge to point out that I don't *want* to settle down, that Sadie's suspension is a perfect reason for me to have some nonsettled emotions.

Instead, I turn to Keenan. "We have to find Mr. Darren."

The Verdict

We eat lunch barely speaking, and then I spend free period on the office couch again, and then during passing time before language arts we run for the student lounge. Inside, we find Mr. Darren kneeling in front of a Fender Twin amp. It's turned around backward and he's replacing the tubes and has one of the short glass cylinders in his hand.

He sees us and says, "Hey, Mr. Armstrong, Mr. Jones, how can I help you?"

"Did you hear that Sadie got suspended?" Keenan asks.

Mr. Darren sighs. "I did."

"Can she do the show?" I ask, even though I know it's useless.

"I'm afraid not," says Mr. Darren. "This is considered a school activity, and with her suspension she'll miss our last two practices, so . . . There you go."

I can feel myself starting to shake with frustration. "So, what are we going to do?"

Mr. Darren kind of shrugs. "Well, I'm not sure. Sadie's the singer for the Random Sample too." He's talking about the seventh grade band. "I was thinking maybe both bands could learn cover songs and Eric from the Bespin Mining Guild could sing"—that's the sixth grade band—"but I think that might be too much to put on his plate."

He smiles sadly at us. "We may just need to plan ahead for the spring show. I mean, we have a good start on the tune. And more time is never a bad thing."

"This sucks!" mutters Keenan. He's staring at the ground with his hands shoved in his pockets like he does when he's mad.

"Why did Sadie have to be such an idiot?" I add.

"Well, I'm sure she didn't mean to sabotage the band," says Mr. Darren. "But in rock and roll, it's all about timing, and there is this weird correlation between big shows and the craziest things happening." Mr. Darren laughs a little when he says this, but it's weary, like he's been through it.

The afternoon bell sounds and Mr. Darren writes us a pass to LA. Keenan and I are silent as we walk there. There's no use saying anything. It feels like when you're standing near a mine blast in *LF* and for a few seconds you stagger and the sound gets distant and everything is hidden by clouds of smoke. And then you look down and see that half your leg is gone, and the screen goes red. Game over.

The Last Place in the World
I Want to Be

When we walk into LA, Ms. Rosaz has already started the lesson. I throw my junk on my table and drop into my chair. I know it's a distraction but right now I don't even care.

"Anthony and Keenan, you should have your books and writer's notebooks out on your desks," says Ms. Rosaz, annoyed by our disruption but of course not bothering to ask what we might be upset about. "The rest of the class has already started."

I huff and dig into my bag for the paperback book and drop it on my desk, then slap open my binder and pull out my writer's notebook. Every movement I make is loud and Ms. Rosaz is probably going to snap any second. Whatever.

There's no way I can focus right now. I can't believe we're not going to get to play Arts Night! And April is forever from now. Everything we've been dreaming of for the entire fall just got snatched away from us.

I stare out the window thinking about this, thinking about what's *not* going to happen: being onstage with our amps and our guitars and rocking the new tune with my new part and feeling that feeling of playing for everyone again. It was so awesome last year.

So when Ms. Rosaz taps me on the shoulder I can't even begin to answer her question mainly because I didn't hear it. "What?" I say, glancing quickly at the board and trying to read the assignment on the projector screen.

I'm not that good at hearing assignments the first time anyway, because I'm usually just thinking about other stuff. There was talk, back in like fourth grade, of putting me on one of those Learning Plans, where the psychologist tests you and you get pulled out to the resource room for whatever torture goes on there, but it never happened. I guess I started doing just well enough to not be considered *that* dumb. And by this point in school, I've figured out how to catch up with what's going on really quick.

"Please, get started," says Ms. Rosaz.

"I don't feel like it," I tell her, partly because it's the truth, not that she cares what I'm really going through, but also because I don't know what we're doing yet.

"Anthony," she says in *that tone*. "This is something you could do well on. I'd like to see you at least give it a shot." She pats me on the shoulder and walks away. It usually takes her about five minutes to circle the room, and so by the time she gets back and I tell her that I can't think of anything, I should probably at least figure out what we're supposed to be thinking about.

My table-mate is Clara. She's one of those kids who look like they could get hired tomorrow to run a law firm or brief a crack commando unit on behalf of a top-secret agency. She's not a cute-bot, more like a success-bot. She has trendy black rectangle glasses with red trim. Her hair is perfectly wound up behind her head. She always wears button-downs and jeans or long skirts and always this black fleece jacket, the kind that's ready for a rain shower or a quick infiltration of a mountain hideout. She's the kind of girl who loves writing and loves having teachers love her and she's sitting there right now with her pen zipping down the back side of the page she's already completed of whatever it is we're supposed to be doing.

"Hey," I whisper. "What are we doing?"

Clara keeps writing, but with her free hand she flips around her copy of the book we've been reading in class called *Feed* by an author named M. T. Anderson who I've never heard of.

It's about these kids with chips in their heads so that all these ads and stuff are being broadcast right into their brains. The kids are annoying. They use all these weird words because it's supposed to be set in the future. And the narrator is kind of an idiot, which is also annoying. The book is maybe kinda interesting, though, especially when the main girl, Violet, starts to die and the main guy, Titus, gets freaked out. Also, the story is about resisting the Feed, which is kind of like resisting food corporations.

"We're supposed to write our own definitive list of things we want to do," Clara says, "based on this chapter."

I see the page number and open my copy and check it out. It's a pretty cool part. I haven't actually read this far yet but I've heard the discussions in class. Violet is sick and so she's lying in the hospital dreaming of what she wishes her life would be like, even though it's pretty obvious that she's totally gonna die. The list she makes is kind of ridiculous, but interesting. Like she wants to fly over a volcano and spit in it, and run away with Titus, but she also wants things like to be seen by her grandchildren while wearing a cardigan sweater, have a dog named Paine, and to move to an East Coast city for a job, and Ms. Rosaz pointed out that the list has this kind of sad tone to it because you know she probably won't survive to ever do any of the things on it.

"Thanks," I whisper to Clara.

I open my notebook and write down the title but then just stare at the page. Right away I think about how I could write about the New York dream: how Keenan and I imagine practicing in some crappy warehouse where there's bands on all sides and it smells like old beer and stale cigarettes and the bathroom stalls have no doors and are always splattered with puke. Or playing all-ages clubs on Tuesday nights and working our way up and then doing really well like Mr. Darren did with Tender. Touring all across the country in a black van with a matching trailer full of gear. Like to the Midwest, riding the interstates from Kansas City to Detroit to St. Louis and then Chicago because that would be a cool tour if you look on a map. . . .

But what would be the point of writing about that now? We can't even play the one stupid gig we have! I should just face it: none of those dreams are ever going to happen. It occurs to me that this would make me similar to the character Violet, both dreaming of impossible things. Maybe that was fun for her to write about, but it sounds totally depressing to me.

And then before I can figure out what to do, Ms. Rosaz is already back behind me. "Ooh, Clara, that's really cool," she says in that tone that she uses to sound like she's *just one of the kids* and *so* interested, even though about half the time she actually looks like she's going to fall asleep on her feet in class. I glance over and see that Clara is basically on her six thousandth page.

Ms. Rosaz looks at my blank page. "Anthony, you need to get some writing done on this assignment."

I feel like saying, *Duh!* But instead I say, "I was just thinking of what to write," because it's true.

"You look like you're just staring off into space," she says.

"I was thinking," I say again, and now I sound annoyed because I am! Would it be so hard for her to notice that I'm having a terrible day, or maybe even to wonder what I might be going through? Of course not. Or at least just take the hint and leave me alone?

"I know you can do this," she goes on, like I'm a toddler. "Come on, we still have some class time left. Try to get at least five things."

She leaves and I look at my blank page. Even if I did have anything right now, the last thing I'd want to do is share it with Ms. Rosaz, who wouldn't really care anyway. But she says I just need to write five things and time is ticking by, so I just write some junk:

Definitive List of Things
I Want to Do

1. Own a Lamborghini because <u>Every Weapon Needs a Master</u>.
2. Be done with this list.
3. For class to be over.
4. Have enough time to figure out what I <u>actually</u> wish for, now that what I really want is NOT HAPPENING.
5. Have a different life.

Whatever

Then I go back to staring out the window and thinking about how far away spring is. How I now have to spend five more months of slow eighth grade torture waiting for my next chance to be who I really am.

When Ms. Rosaz returns, she looms over my shoulder and reads my list. I can practically hear her eyes narrowing in frustration. "Anthony," she says, "this is an unacceptable effort."

"What?" I say. "You said five things. That's five things."

"'Every weapon needs a master'?"

"That's what the Lamborghini website says! Look it up!"

"This is really all you wish for?"

I want to tell her, *Obviously not, read number four! I have giant wishes but they're not going to happen! And I thought about doing it like that but you didn't give me time. . . .*

But what's the point? So I just say, "Yep."

It comes out pretty obnoxious. I know it does. But I feel like, whatever.

Keenan is two tables over and he hears me and it makes him laugh. And that makes a laugh bubble up in me. As it's happening I know what it's going to lead to but I can't help it. Suddenly I'm laughing and everything feels hilarious, or pointless, or maybe those are the same right now but I can't stop the urge.

"Okay, Anthony, that's enough," says Ms. Rosaz. "Now you're distracting others. You're getting a zero for class participation today. Please leave the room and finish your work in the library or you'll get a zero for the assignment too."

"Why do I need to leave?" I ask, but I can't help cracking up a little more. And this makes Keenan laugh even harder, and then I'm going off more too and I swear I don't know why that happens sometimes, it just does! And I know I should stop but it also feels like a huge relief, like it's the only way to cope with this dumb situation, even though I know how mad it's making Ms. Rosaz.

Clara is leaning back and pulling her notebook closer to her, like she's terrified that my bad-student disease might spread to her.

Ms. Rosaz raises her voice. "Because you're not doing your work and you're being a disruption to the class—"

I cut her off, though, because now everyone in class is

watching and who even cares? I have no ground left to defend, so why not just say what's really on my mind? "If you had just left me alone it would be fine!" I say, but I am also grabbing all my stuff and heading for the door because honestly the library sounds way better than being here.

I hear Ms. Rosaz sigh, another person exhausted by Anthony. "It's the end of the week and neither of us wants me to send an email home about this. This assignment is being graded, so I still need you to get it done," she says to my back as I walk out, as if I didn't hear her the first *hundred* times she mentioned it, like I'm deaf or something.

Under my breath, I mutter what I really think of this assignment.

Meron and Katie are the only ones close enough to hear what I actually say, and it makes them sit up, and Meron says, "Ooh!"

"Anthony, please tell me I didn't just hear what I think I heard," barks Ms. Rosaz from across the room.

I spin around. "What?" I say, playing innocent.

"That is not School-Appropriate Language," she says.

But I have had *enough* of everything and so I say right back, "Who cares about 'School Appropriate'?" I make air quotes around the words. "You guys treat us like we're in kindergarten!"

I can tell that I have Ms. Rosaz really fired up because her eyes kind of bug out and actually my heart is racing now too but it's too late because we are in it.

"It is school policy," she says, trying to keep her cool, but I can tell she wants to just let loose and scream at me, "not because you are kindergartners but because that kind of language can be hurtful."

"I didn't say anything!" I reply. I should stop there . . . "But if I did," I keep going, "so what? I heard that scientists found out that swearing is good for you because it helps you feel better faster." This makes Katie and Meron and Keenan and a couple of other kids totally crack up even more, but it's actually true! I overheard my dad telling my mom about the article and I looked it up. "It was in *Scientific American*," I say, "and last time I checked, *Scientific American* was way more official than the Catharine Daly Student Conduct Code."

"Okay, Anthony!" Ms. Rosaz yells, so furious that her voice cracks. "Library." She shoos me away with this look on her face like, why did she ever get into teaching in the first place?

"Fine."

Lyrics

I go to the library and Ms. Daniels points me to a table. At first I just sit there and steam because Ms. Rosaz sucks! Why couldn't she just give me a chance? And then she totally dismissed my point about swears!

These teachers are all the same. I think the *real* reason *they* don't let us swear is because they're scared of us kids being able to fully express ourselves, and they don't want us to have all the tools at our disposal because then maybe we'd be able to fight back and make our points. Maybe then we'd be too strong for them. We'd overwhelm the prison guards and take over.

Though maybe I *was* making a scene in class. But it didn't have to go like that! She could have just left me alone.

After a while I calm down. I think about maybe doing the stupid assignment, but I still don't feel like it. I end up doodling, drawing *The Rusty Soles* in metallic lettering, but that makes me think about Sadie and Arts Night again and there's really nothing left to think about with that sucky topic.

I put my head down on the desk and zone out. After a few minutes, my thoughts return to the song. It runs along in my brain, Killer G to Flying Aces. I compare it to some of the bands I like, like the Kneebacks or Green Day II. Then I realize that the song sounds the most like something by SilentNoize. I can kinda hear Jake Diamond in my head and now I start to wonder what kind of melody he would sing over it. I try to imagine him singing, and I start to hear a melody floating over the tune. And more, I hear some words.

I start scribbling them down before I forget.

> You always tell me what I need to do
> You always tell me how I need to be

I work on making the rhythms similar, and the rhyming . . .

> You think that I should listen to you
> When you don't care what's important to me

When I look up I find that almost ten minutes have gone by like nothing. I look back at the lyrics:

Whoa, those are kinda good. And they fit the melody just right. Lyrics to our song. This is pretty cool. When I've written lyrics before, they've never felt this . . . complete. Or serious.

Real feeling is what I mean. Honest.

And wait, if I have lyrics, then . . . could I sing them? I mean, maybe I could. Sing them. If I wrote more. And we need a singer. . . .

Could that be me?

Then we could still play Arts Night. With me lead-singing. I wouldn't be replacing Sadie or taking over the band. It could just be this one time.

The thought makes me nervous. Or maybe excited. It's like both.

The bell sounds. I head out of the library quick. We're already a few minutes into social studies before I realize that I probably should have gone back to LA after class and showed Ms. Rosaz what I wrote. Except I didn't actually write anything. And she didn't even come find me at the end of class so it probably doesn't matter. It's Friday afternoon anyway. She probably didn't follow up on it because she wants to get to the weekend just as much as me.

One more class and I can get out of here and figure out if these lyrics would really work, and if we have a chance to save Arts Night.

Activist Blues

The day ends and Keenan and Skye and I are headed into the center of Ballard when it starts to rain hard. I haven't told them about the lyrics yet. I'd tell Keenan if it was just the two of us, but when is it ever anymore?

Also, over the past hour, my excitement about the words has been turned down a few notches by doubt. How could I really sing onstage and pull off playing guitar? And how do I know those lyrics are even any good? They might be totally stupid.

Part of me is still a little worried that Ms. Rosaz sent an email home about our fight in class, like she threatened. It would be some kind of stupid luck if the very day that I maybe find a way to save Arts Night, I get in trouble at home and lose the chance to play it in the first place.

The wind kicks up as we walk, and it starts pouring. None of us have umbrellas, because everybody knows you do *not* use an umbrella in Seattle, and Keenan and Skye are huddled under his jacket, which leaves me walking basically alone. The rain feels like strafing fire from the Normandy beachhead and I need a raincoat like a GI needs a sulfa packet, but of course I'm just in my sweatshirt again and somewhere Rosalie is shaking her head.

Our plan is to get mochas, but we haven't decided where yet, and now it's so wet and we are passing the first Starbucks, so I say, "Let's just go in here."

But Skye is like, "No. Way. We are not going into the evil corporate beast."

"It's pouring!" I say.

"Oh, okay," Skye snaps, throwing up her arms, "then after this, why don't we just hop on a plane and go to the developing world and kill some babies? Because that would basically be the same thing."

See what I mean? *Ninja!*

Keenan just laughs, maybe because he knows what she's saying is crazy. On a different day, I might join him. Instead all I can do is scowl.

"What—it's true!" Skye snaps at him.

"They also wouldn't display your Winky donation jar," Keenan points out.

"Fine!" I say, all extra loud. Ugh! I feel like pointing out that everything we're wearing and our backpacks and probably the air we're breathing was all made in a developing country so what's the point of deciding that of all the criminal corporations, you're going to boycott Starbucks? Why couldn't it be somewhere else that's maybe less convenient to our walk home in this sucky weather?

It's another three blocks of bitter rain before we get to

Jupiter, the indie coffee shop that's all about how they only buy beans that were grown responsibly in the shade of a rain forest surrounded by toucans and geckos, and no, no fossil fuels are ever used and yes, all the profits go to saving whales. And all that leads to mochas that are kinda silty. Skye says that's just because they're more *real*, but that's the annoying thing about *real* and the reason why *fake* was invented in the first place. There would have been no silt at the evil Starbucks.

But Jupiter does have good baked stuff. And with everything I'm feeling inside, I add a chocolate-chip espresso muffin to my order. It's not what I should do. It's giving in to the blood sugar saboteurs. And yes, I know that the biggest danger with junk food is to use it like comfort food to make you feel better, and I *know*, just like the food scientists do, that all the sugar and sodium can trip you out like any other drug and on and on, but I also know that knowing all that is not going to stop me from getting an espresso muffin right now, because it is going to rock and I am just not going to tell my parents.

We sit down on a couch along the wall. Skye joins us a second later, after grabbing the Winky donation jar that Jupiter let her put by the counter. It's a glass jar taped to a small poster with a photo of Winky on Meron's finger and a brief explanation of his situation written in bright pink. She pulls a single dollar out, then tips the jar to pour out the coins.

"So," says Skye as she does this, "what are you guys gonna do now that Sadie's—"

"Watch out!" I shout, because from my angle I can see—

The mocha sludge lurking on the bottom of the jar, which

pours onto Skye's hand and down into her lap. It's not much, like someone dumped their silty leftovers in there, obviously to be a jerk. Dark blotches stain Skye's jeans. She gazes down at the soaked quarters and pennies in her palm, then glares around the room.

"Hipsters are hypocrites," she mutters.

Keenan darts up for napkins. "A couple people donated," he says when he gets back, in classic boyfriend mode.

"I bet if Winky was a panda you'd have like a thousand dollars," I add, in less helpful ex-boyfriend mode and also maybe because I'm still annoyed at my extra level of wet from walking here.

But then I feel bad because Skye is actually crying as she dabs at her jeans. "You try to make a difference," she says, "to stand up for someone without a voice, and . . . somebody does this."

I almost point out that this someone without a voice is just a sparrow but I know enough to know better. Also, I'm halfway through my muffin and the pure bomb of sugar is smoothing over my thoughts like a knife over frosting.

"So yeah, Mr. Darren says we probably have to wait until the Spring Arts Night," says Keenan, once Skye seems to have cooled off. "Sadie might be kicked out of Rock Band Club permanently too, which means we'll need a new singer." He sounds really disappointed.

And then, maybe it's just the sugar talking, but I hear myself saying . . . "Maybe not." I dig through my backpack and yank out my writer's notebook. Even as I'm doing this I feel a wicked sword of nerves stab up from my guts. Am I really going to show them?

"What do you mean?" Keenan asks.

"I, um . . ." I flip to the lyrics. Yes, I'm gonna do it. "Here, look at this."

First Look

Keenan and Skye study my notebook. "*That's* what you wrote for the wish list?" says Skye, seeing my lame list from class. She starts to laugh. "No wonder Ms. Rosaz was pissed."

"Not that part." I point below. "Here."

"What's that?" Keenan asks.

"Is it a poem?" Skye asks.

"No. Lyrics," I say, feeling a flash of heat and cold sweat at the same time. "Like, for the Killer G song. Maybe."

"Oh . . . ," says Keenan. I can't tell if it's the good "oh" or the bad one. "Well, how do they go?"

"What do you mean?"

"Ooh, yeah," says Skye. It's like the two of them have been going out for so long that they've grown a uni-brain. "Sing it for us!"

"No!" I say. "But what do you think of them?"

"I don't know," says Keenan. "They could be pretty cool, I guess. Have you tried them out on the tune?"

"No. I just wrote them." I can't tell: is Keenan asking because he'd want that or not?

But then he says, "Record them tonight and send me the file. I'll put bass on it. If it's cool we could even put it on Band-Space." He sounds like he means it.

"No, we're not doing *that*," I say, the nerve sword stabbing again. We put a BandSpace page together for the Rusty Soles last year. All it has is the live recording of our song from the Spring Arts Night last year. We got like thirty-five plays and ten downloads, which isn't much but it was fun, although I think eight or nine of those downloads were our parents. Still, I am not ready to have my singing out there where anyone in the world could hear it.

"But," I say, "I mean, if the words sound okay . . . I could try to do them for Arts Night."

I wonder if Keenan will be bothered by this idea, because it would be me doing too much . . . but his eyes light up. "We could still play!" he says. "The Rusty Soles are back!"

"Well, not definitely," I say, and I feel my face getting red. "Just, maybe . . ." I am feeling crazy inside, like, *Yes!* because again, this could happen, we could still play the show. I could sing, and the band would be complete!

Keenan is still smiling, but then his eyes kind of widen as he looks over my shoulder. "Hey, look!" he whispers to us, nodding his chin toward the door.

I turn and see that Valerie and her friend Lena have just walked in.

Moment of Truth

I turn back around, trying to keep my cool.

But Skye's girl radar immediately notices. "No way!" she says. "Anthony likes Valerie?" She makes this face that is one of the most annoying faces that an ex-girlfriend who's still your friend can make. It's that smiley, knowing, *I've seen you act like that about me* look.

"Shut up," I mutter.

"He totally does," says Keenan, also grinning. "She's a really good drummer."

He means it in my defense but then Skye turns to him with the raised eyebrow in full effect. "So what, you're in love with her too?"

"Duh, no!" says Keenan, but Skye is pulling her arm back and that makes him spill his mocha a little. "Ugh," he says. He glances over my shoulder again. "She's coming this way."

Suddenly I'm feeling completely unprepared, like, are my shoes tied? And is my fly up? And are my hoodie straps caught in my collar or anything?

"Hey, guys." Valerie and Lena arrive beside us. When you're sitting, Valerie really is pretty tall and she's kinda looming over us. She is wearing this cool vintage wool coat that's oversized and probably for a guy, and a knitted purple hat with snowflakes on it and her black hair is coming out of it in two braids. I am noticing these things and thinking again that she is probably cute, which is obviously why Keenan and Skye have these *jerk*-big smiles on their faces. I also realize that the clock is ticking since she said hi and I haven't said anything yet and I need to *say something*.

"Hey," I say, and that's it and I say it totally normal but still I hear Keenan snicker quietly and I consider deforming his face with my mocha. Then I say to Valerie, "Did you hear about Sadie?"

Valerie's mouth scrunches like she's disappointed. It's sorta cute. "Yeah," she says. "So, I guess we're kinda screwed."

"Anthony wrote some lyrics!" Keenan practically shouts.

I turn to him and try to make sure he understands that the look I give him for a split second says, *You are a dead man*. It was one thing to show him and Skye . . .

But then Valerie says, "Oh wow, really? Anthony, you write lyrics too?"

"Well," I say, "sometimes. I mean . . . this time I did." My pulse is starting to sprint.

"They're for the Rusty Soles," says Keenan like he's my agent or something. "He's going to sing them and we can still play the show."

Valerie gets this big grin that makes her eyes kinda squint. "Can I see them?"

"Uh," I say, and for a second I just sit there like I'm a frozen screen, my operating system stuck on the idea. *You can't really show her, you don't know if they're that great, or what she'll think, or—*

But then Keenan says, "Here," and just grabs my notebook and hands it over.

I know it would be ridiculous to snatch it back. "There,"

I say, pointing to the right spot on the page. Then I glare at Keenan again. I kinda want to kill him. He smiles at me like he thinks he did me a huge favor. Okay, maybe he did.

Valerie's eyes scan down the page. Still reading . . . It seems to take her longer than it should. Too long. I sit there wondering, *What will she think? What is she thinking? What did she already think? Did she think they were stupid and now she's buying time trying to think of a good lie?*

Another second passes.

Okay, yes, she definitely thought they were garbage.

I wish I hadn't showed her.

Then she finally looks up. "They're really good," she says, and even though I hear her, it takes me a second to realize that she actually sounds like she means it.

She is looking at me and I notice that her eyes are really big and dark brown. A little bit like a shark's, but in a good way. That's probably not something I should tell her, ever.

"I mean, this would be a cool song," Valerie says. "Are you going to write more?"

"Yeah," I say, trying to make it sound like *of course* I'm going to write more, that it's just a matter of selecting the perfect words for the deep artistic vision I clearly have and you can't rush these things.

"Cool," she says, and smiles at me.

I smile back.

We are smiling.

And then a second passes and nobody has said anything and suddenly it's awkward, like we're stuck in this smiling position and neither of us knows what to do next. I can feel Keenan and Skye working their couple-spreading spells behind me, like if I turn around I will find them wiggling their fingers and wearing floppy wizard hats. And I can feel myself starting to sweat because I have no idea what to say next. There has to be something. . . .

Then I see Lena nudge Valerie with her elbow, and Valerie makes this little surprised face, and then she says, "Oh hey, it's Friday." It almost seems like she's going to stop there, which would be really strange, but then she adds, "Are you guys doing anything tonight?"

"Um," I say. If there was a heart-rate meter bar beside me like in *Liberation Force* it would be spiking with all the red bars lit and I would be looking for a chunk of blasted wall to crouch behind and build my strength back up and hopefully there'd be a med kit there too, but here in Jupiter Coffee there's no cover.

"Because," Valerie continues, "there's a show down at the Vera Project tonight. Have you heard of Fractured Senses?"

"Ooh, yeah," says Keenan. "They're pretty cool."

I shoot him a look that says that answer was *mine*. He shrugs.

"They're playing with the Clones and Lost Puppy," Valerie continues. "Lena's brother is in Lost Puppy. They're good."

"Nice," I say.

"Well, anyway, um, we'll be there," Valerie finishes, and suddenly it gets quiet again.

I am just kind of sitting there, screen still frozen, when

suddenly I realize that *duh*, this is an invitation. "Oh," I say, a little too loudly. "Well, yeah, we, um, we could maybe do that too." I turn to Keenan and Skye. "What do you think? Wanna go?" I ask, nodding slightly at Keenan.

Keenan says, "Sure," except then when he looks at Skye she scowls and looks away. Poor Keenan, he thought they were still in couple-magic mode, but it's obvious from Skye's face that she had something else in mind for tonight, so that's going to be a whole big thing, but who cares? They've been dating for forever. She can deal.

"Great," says Valerie. "So . . . maybe we'll see you there?"

"Yeah," I say, "definitely."

There is *another* silent second and then Valerie kind of shrugs and her mouth moves like she's telling herself something and then she says, "Well, bye," and they walk away.

"See you later," I say.

When I turn back around I am smiling. And a mess: I notice my sweaty palms and a light-headed feeling. Either this is one giant sugar rush or . . . I am pretty into Valerie. More than I'd even thought about.

I mean, other than Skye, my only other girlfriend ever was Elana and that started at last year's spring dance when we were dancing to "Torn Socket" by the Kneebacks, and it ended fifty-two minutes later when she sent Clara to break up with me while I was standing in the drink line. So, this is feeling like something.

Definitely something.

I would revel in this girl-success moment with Keenan a bit, except he is busy doing damage control with Skye, who is slouched and pouty about whatever she had on her mind to do tonight. She probably told him and he just spaced, and she should understand that he was just trying to help out his best friend, but knowing Skye, she'll be mad for days.

I look down at my notebook, at the lyrics, and consider that maybe a crappy week like this one is actually going to end in victory. Lyrics, Arts Night saved, and a date! With a killer drummer. For once, it feels like I have the timing right.

Blitzkrieg

On the way home we agree to ask our parents about going down to Vera. Well, Keenan and I agree. Skye is silent. And poor Keenan has to talk to me in that low, I'm-in-the-doghouse way so he doesn't make things worse. We plan to text about meeting there around seven. My parents never have a problem with me going to Vera, because it's all-ages and a nonprofit and all that.

I spend the rest of the walk to my house buzzing about tonight, about hanging out with Valerie, but I am also excited to get home and get in a couple hours working on Killer G and trying out the lyrics and melody that are suddenly real.

I'm almost to my house before I remember the whole thing

with Ms. Rosaz. Did she send an email home, or was she too tired to bother? I bet she let it go. Friday, weekend, and what I did wasn't even a big deal so whatever.

Inside, Erica is watching some annoying movie about a girl who by day is a high school student but by night is some kind of space-traveling princess. She has a sidekick who's something like a sardine crossed with a stalk of broccoli and wears sunglasses and it's like . . . who even knows where all these show ideas come from? I'm glad I was little during the age of cartoons that were cool and actually made sense, like *SpongeBob*.

Mom is in the dining room, which is also the office. I grab my waiting plate of stalag rations. Today we have nonfat cottage cheese and grapes and kiwi slices and nine almonds.

I head straight for my room and just call out, "Hey, Mom, gonna practice and then I'm gonna go to Vera tonight for a show at seven. I don't need a ride, I can take the bus, okay? Cool." I'm starting up the stairs as I finish.

There is no answer right away. All is quiet on the front. . . .

But I am only a few steps up when Mom says, "Anthony!" and the tone of her voice is like the distant rumble of panzers in the peaceful valleys of the Ardennes. (That's part of the movie intro to *LF*, where the Germans ran a blitzkrieg through exactly the one place the French thought they wouldn't because it was this really forested area.)

I stop. "Yeah?"

"Come down here."

"What?" I huff and turn around and head into the dining room, trying to sound like I couldn't possibly know what's up.

The farmer stands at the banks of the gently curving Meuse, herding his dairy cattle for a drink at the water's edge. On the other side of the wide river, old trees stretch to steep mountains, the border of Belgium. Wind shakes them and for a second he wonders if he just heard the rumble of machinery.

Mom looks up at me with the blue glow of her laptop reflecting against her glasses and does she look mad? Or just tired? It's still possible that we'll be okay here.

"That's cool about Vera tonight, right?" I ask innocently.

"Anthony."

There is another rumble, but it's probably just thunder and that's fine because his fields could use the rain. The cows bump around each other and their bells jangle. Nearby, the farmer's neighbor is plowing his champagne vineyard. Spring birds sing in the trees and the river gurgles. It was probably nothing. . . .

And yet I know what's coming.

"Care to explain what happened in English class today?"

Bam! *The trees blast apart and the great mechanized beasts lunge over the bank and into the river, their toothy tracks churning the water into mud.*

"What?" I say, trying to sound like I have no idea what she's talking about.

"I got an email from Ms. Rosaz," says Mom, "informing me that you mouthed off and got sent out of class, and then on top of that you didn't even turn in your writing work."

The tanks run up the bank. The farmer tries to herd the cows to safety, but they scatter and some drown and others are mashed to hamburger beneath the giant clutching tracks. The tanks blow through the old walls that were used as defenses as far back as Charlemagne, scattering the rocks like a child's plastic blocks.

"Mom!" I say, and even though I knew there was a chance of this, I still can't believe it, and I feel like what I say next is true. "That's so unfair!" Because it's not like I send emails to Principal Tiernan whenever Ms. Rosaz gives us a boring lesson or a dumb assignment or yawns while someone is reading in class! And I know my defenses aren't going to hold, I know I'm no match for the email blitzkrieg, but I have to try.

"She didn't give me a chance to get started," I say. "And I was only late because we were talking to Mr. Darren about how Sadie got suspended. And then I *did* the work, the stupid list thing, I did it! But she told me it wasn't good enough anyway."

"She said you were causing a disruption in class," says Mom, her voice low like she's trying to keep her cool, "and that you used inappropriate language."

"No, she's the one who caused the disruption!" I'm starting to shout but I can't help it. "'Cause she sent me out of class even though I did the work!"

"Anthony"—I can hear the frustration building in her voice—"this is twice in two days!"

"She hates me, Mom!" I say. "She's got her favorites like Clara and they can do whatever they want but then I get singled out!" And I feel like that's a little bit true. I mean, does

Ms. Rosaz honestly like me as much as Clara? There's no way. And I know this argument isn't going to work either, but at this point the tanks are rolling on toward Sedan and nobody knows they're coming and I am just standing there in cow guts.

"Oh, come on," says Mom. "Ms. Rosaz does not hate you. And how much reason are you giving her to *like* you, Anthony?"

"She didn't even care that I'd basically just had my year ruined!"

"She has thirty other kids to worry about. And what are you talking about?"

"Sadie got suspended and now we can't play Arts Night!"

"Well . . ." This causes a crack in Mom's anger. "Did you tell any of this to Ms. Rosaz?"

"No," I say, "but she wouldn't care anyway!" I hear myself shouting, and I hate this! I feel bad for giving Mom a hard time, for the tired look I can see in her eyes, but what else am I supposed to do? "Whatever, it's just dumb!" I realize that I should probably stop, that I still need to think about my lyrics, about saving Arts Night, if it's not already too late, but I can't. "And besides, the thing we had to do was stupid!"

"Well, it's too bad you feel that way," says Mom, "because I let Ms. Rosaz know that you'd be turning that assignment in on Monday and that it would be your best effort. She agreed to give you half credit."

"Oh," I snap, "so you guys are all buddies now, like the Axis?"

"The what?" Mom shrugs. "Anthony, you weren't able to make the right decision in the moment so—"

"Whatever," I mutter, and start out of the room.

But Mom doesn't let me go as easy as she did yesterday. "You can get started on it tonight because you won't be leaving the house."

I spin around. "What? Come on! I'm grounded?"

"No, you're getting the work done that you should have done this afternoon. And you are not going to the Vera Project. We can talk later about whether there need to be more consequences for this."

I glare at her, all the feelings boiling over, like I hate her, like I hate Ms. Rosaz, everyone . . . but I don't say anything else. Just storm out. I think about throwing my plate of stalag food across the room. But I don't do that either. Just pound my feet on each step as I head for my room, and when I get there I slam the door and then I just sit on my bed.

I stare at the wall. I make fists until my nails dig into my palms, and then I release them and make them again. I can't move, don't want to move, don't want to think. And I feel like there is no way out for me, ever. Out of this house, this life.

Nothing ever, *ever* works out.

Aftermath

I hear Dad get home.

I hear *them* talking.

Mom calls up to me for dinner. I don't go down. I figure she'll call again, but she doesn't bother.

A little while later, there's a knock and Dad opens my door. He's got a plate of Thai stir-fry with tofu. He hands it to me, and as he's stepping out he says, "Please just get that work done this evening so we can put this behind us."

"It's dumb," I say, almost wishing I could stop myself, but who even cares?

"Anthony . . ."

"Fine."

I eat in silence, all the lights off except for this one desk lamp that's got a red lightbulb.

I text Keenan and let him know I can't go to Vera and I tell him to let Valerie know what happened when he sees her. He doesn't text me back. He's probably dealing with mad Skye or, knowing him, his battery is dead. Whatever.

I am thinking about opening my window and climbing out, wondering like I have a bunch of times before about how much it would hurt to drop down onto the deck from my window. Probably a lot, but maybe I'd get lucky and just sprain an ankle, and that would be worth it. Or maybe I'd be too heavy and break a board on the deck and that would definitely give me away. Then I am thinking about just storming down the stairs, right past my parents and out to do what I want.

But I don't do any of those things. I don't break plates. I don't run out on my own. Because what would be the point? Anything I do is just going to get me in more trouble and more trapped in this stupid stalag that is my life.

After a while I open the Rock Star app on my phone, the music-recording program that Keenan and I use. I plug in a headphone/microphone splitter, then my earbuds and a Sure microphone (just an SM57, because Mr. Darren says if you can't make it sound good on an SM57 it probably doesn't sound good anyway). I hang the mic by its cord over my desk chair. Then I place the little HoneyTone right beneath it. I set up a preset drum loop in the program that sounds stupid but is just enough like what Valerie is playing on Killer G, and I sit on the floor against my bed and plug in Merle.

I start the beat and then hit Record, playing Killer G to Flying Aces, looping the two parts a couple times. Playing calms me down, pushes away the angry walls, just my fingers and the pick and the strings snapping beneath it—

There's a knock at the door. Mom's voice from the other side: "You should be working on your list."

My only answer is to kick Merle's case. It slams into the chair. The microphone falls down with a thud. Great. Can't even play guitar.

I move to my bed and sit there. I lay Merle beside me and pull out my stupid writer's notebook and look at the list assignment. There is no way I am working on this. They may have me locked up in solitary confinement, but I will not bend to their propaganda.

Beneath it are the lyrics from this afternoon. I think about how they remind me of SilentNoize. I sing them again in my head:

> You always tell me what I need to do
> You always tell me how I need to be
> You think that I should listen to you
> When you don't care what's important to me

The melody I heard in the library is right back in my head. The words feel like a relief. They feel *true*. I think about today, this sucky night, this stupid week, and then suddenly more words are coming to me and I just grab a pen and go.

"Breakout" Is Born

> You say I'm flying out of control
> You say I can't do anything right
> But you don't know what I can really do
> And you don't want me to put up a fight

The rhythm of the syllables maybe isn't perfect but who cares. I keep going:

> A hundred people tell me what to do
> A hundred more say, do what you're told
> I'm like a rat inside this maze of life
> Already dying when I'm barely old

I look up and see that time did that weird thing again where it's almost a half hour later. I look back at what I have. I like it. I can picture the video: something like a World War II flying part for that second verse, and then like a giant maze with huge animated rats for the third verse, all red-eyed. I could fight them off with a katana sword.

I pick up Merle and strum real quiet in my lap, humming the words over it. They all seem like verses and they all fit what I'm hearing for the Killer G part. So, what's going to happen in the Flying Aces section? I play those chords and try each of the verses over them but they don't really fit. That part needs something different.

But my brain is racing along now and I remember how there are those tunes, like by SilentNoize or Arcade Fire, that don't do the usual song structure where you go back and forth between the verse and chorus. Instead, they just stay on one part for a while, repeating and slowly building each time through, and then finally you switch to the second part for the big ending and you stay there and that's the song. My dad says U2 did that the best. Maybe that could work for this.

I have to try it out.

Downstairs I hear Dad washing the dishes. Closer, Erica is taking a shower, and Mom could be lurking anywhere out there.

I put down Merle and grab my phone. I take the recording I'd made before Mom stopped me and I start cutting up the guitar track. I take the Killer G section and paste it four times in a row, then stick the Flying Aces section after that. I set up the drum loop so it doesn't start until the third time through Killer G. For those first two times, I add only a kick drum that is beating on the quarter notes.

I think of Valerie doing this and how playing live you could time pulsing stage lights with it, and Valerie would totally rock that, but then I remember how I was going to see her at Vera tonight and I feel the angry bullets starting to fly all over again.

I grab my mic from the floor and pull my comforter over my head so that I am a lump in the corner of the bed and then there in the dark red light I hit Record. I let the first section of Killer G go by and then I start to sing my lyrics with the melody I've been hearing. Really quiet so the prison guards can't hear. I sing my three verses over the second and third and fourth sections of Killer G. They whisper out of my mouth, mumbling and cracking, but it doesn't matter because it's just a demo and Mr. Darren says that when you're inspired all you have to do is get the golden nugget of an idea down as complete as you can and don't worry about the sounds or the perfection because the only thing that matters is getting that pure inspiration before it's gone.

I rerecord the verses a couple times, until they really sound right. Then I listen back. It's cool. It builds. The first verse is kind of whimpery but then the second one is stronger, and the song really feels like *life* feels lately, where things are getting more and more intense, and trapping you.

I keep looping it and do more takes. I'm sweating under

the covers, and the more I sing the lyrics, the angrier I'm getting. It is starting to feel like yesterday when we were playing Killer G and the music and everything suddenly felt overwhelming. This song is tapped into that feeling.

The song *is* that feeling.

My brain spirals like there's a tornado of everything that has been so frustrating and stupid lately. The email. The call home. My parents. Mr. Scher. Sadie. And even Keenan and Skye, not just because of Skye's opinions but also because it's like I lost them both when they started dating.

Every part of my life is enemy territory, and it's like in Level 16 of *LF* when you're on your own in the woods after you escape from Stalag VII-A, and a pack of German dogs is on your scent and they've cornered you in a barn and there is no escape—that's how it feels all the time to be me and to deal with everything and all I can think

all I can think

all I can barely think is

F*** everything!

is honestly how I really feel, but oh no, you can't say that. It's not okay to use *those* words to describe your feelings, the most powerful words, the most accurate. We're supposed to just be perfect and young and *fine* all the time, with no real problems. But we're not fine. And when things really suck, keeping it bottled up inside only makes it worse.

It's like in eighth grade you are too old and too young all at once. And who you feel like you are, and who you're expected to be are just completely opposite and wrong and maybe *that* is what this song is about.

I am having that feeling again like yesterday where this angry energy is showing me something, the hidden door, the secret tunnel in the barn's grain cellar, the way out. . . .

I start the song over but this time I set the recording to go all the way through to the Flying Aces part to see if I can make it build and I don't know what I'm going to do when I get there and I am not going to plan it. At least within these little wavy lines of sound I am going to be free to escape and fly above all of the stupid rules and expectations.

I hit Record and start singing from the top, singing it just like I feel it and I don't care if it sounds dumb or wrong or whatever.

"You always tell me what I need to do . . ."

I sing the first three verses, letting it build, getting more intense. My voice is starting to shake but also getting stronger, angrier.

Then the song changes to the Flying Aces part and I just sprint ahead into it and I feel like I am following something or it is pulling me along or I am pushing it or I have no idea how to describe it better than that and I am practically shouting now and the words just happen and I just *go* . . .

"So I'll tell you what I want
And I'll tell you what I think

And I'll tell you how I feel
Are you ready to listen?
F*** THIS PLACE!
I've gotta break out
F*** THIS PLACE!
We've gotta break out
Break out
Into the sun . . ."

The Monster Unleashed

The music ends. The program keeps recording, hissing in my ears like I'm drifting somewhere out in empty space.

I feel like I've lost track of my body, but then I hear my breathing, fast and raspy. My throat is sore.

And all I can think is *Whoa.*

"Anthony?"

I hear the muffled voice and I throw back my comforter and drop it over my phone and the mic just as my door is opening and I grab my notebook and have it in my lap and there is innocent Anthony, sitting in his bed like a perfect little son making up for the mistakes he made.

Mom peers in. In the low red light, she can't tell that my face is red and I'm sweating. "Were you shouting something?" she asks.

"Just singing to myself while I was working," I say, trying

not to sound out of breath or like my heart is pounding like a stampeding bull.

She is quiet for a second, but then she says, "Okay, we're going to bed. Don't forget you have class at ten tomorrow."

"Right," I say.

"Good night."

"Yup."

Mom closes the door. I am having a weird feeling of being in two different worlds or something. I can feel the adrenaline working its way through my system and it's like this huge relief, this huge relaxing. What just happened? I grab my phone and drag the cursor back to the start of the tune.

I am almost afraid to listen to what I just did, but I also can't wait to hear it because I feel like I barely remember doing it, like it happened to somebody else.

I hit Play.

I hear me singing, in this weird quiet way, and it's all muffled beneath the covers but actually that effect sounds kinda cool. The verses build, and here comes the final part, and then I hear myself singing those last lyrics, shouting with a grit and growl that would make Jake Diamond proud.

And then it gets to the f-bombs and it sounds like something magical or terrible or stupid or perfect but what it does more than anything is give me the chills and then it makes me laugh out loud. I can't help it. It's like a recording of some creature inside me unleashed, some kind of demon or something. Like the sound of my true soul when things are at their worst.

"Take that," I say to nobody.

I listen to it probably ten more times, thinking it's amazing sometimes, but then stupid, but then amazing again. I am shocked, but then psyched, and by the tenth time I have started to think about the obvious fact:

This will never fly for the song for *real*. I mean, obviously these f-bomb lyrics will never work for Arts Night. Sure, it would be totally fine for SilentNoize, or even for Sister's Secret when they're playing at Vera, but not for us.

I try to imagine the look on Mr. Scher's face if he heard this, his eyes getting all bugged out and his mouth dropping open, the parents at the Arts Night covering the ears of their little protozoans. That would actually be *insane*. But whatever. There's no way it can happen.

Still, for tonight the song exists like this and I made this and it's true and nobody can tell me it's *wrong* or do anything about it.

So I highlight the whole track and export it to an MP3 and text it to Keenan with a note that says: *Here's how we bring down the Reich.*

Then I put away my phone and grab *Strummer* magazine and sit back against the wall and read.

It's weird. I feel so calm. And I feel weird about how I'm feeling calm but I also feel okay, like less mad. I'm not really thinking about the week or any of the dumb things or really much about anything.

I sit there reading an article about the sound track for the new WereNinjas! movie that is coming out this summer.

They're calling it an inter-prequel because it takes place within a one-month time gap that happened in the second prequel. That sounds stupid. The guy who wrote the sound track apparently used totally fake digital guitars that he played with a keyboard and that is an idea that's as dumb as the movie itself, but I figure me and Keenan will have to check it out to see how much it sucks and laugh at it.

This is the kind of thing I am thinking about.

The anger is gone.

And then the next thing I know it is four a.m. and I am waking up to find my clothes still on and my light still on and I don't change either and just fall back asleep.

10 DAYS

Basic Training with Sergeant Mike

I wake up to KEXP playing Fractured Senses and I remember that last night I was supposed to see them and Valerie was going to be there. I wish I'd gotten to hang out with her, and I hope she wasn't disappointed, but it all feels like a long time ago.

I look down at the microphone lying on my floor and remember the song and that feels like a long time ago too, almost like a dream. Then I remember the crazy swearing lyrics and that seems like some other person, like watching a character like me in a movie. I wonder what Keenan thought of it but there is no text back from him or any emails and so I get up and put on my sweatpants and hoodie for Fat Class.

Downstairs Mom and Dad are up like they always are because they have forgotten how to sleep in. I am never going to let that happen. For them, the weekend has schedules to be kept, order to be maintained.

There are strawberries and blueberries, nonfat vanilla

yogurt and scrambled egg whites and salsa. I grab some and sit on the couch, where Dad is watching one of his favorite shows, *Fatal Storms!*, on the Disaster Channel. He loves anything about science and specifically all the ways that nature is going to kill us. A lot of it is relevant too, since in Seattle we are right near a giant fault line and a huge volcano. It's crazy to think that we worry about all these little things like writing assignments or even our BMI when at any moment some giant geological event could wipe us out. Then again, if Mount Rainier blew, it would be awesome because we'd be able to see it from our roof.

Mom is doing sudoku, the laundry already in. Neither of them really hassles me until Mom's inner clock goes off and she gives me a ride over to the gym where the class is held.

When we got the prediabetes news last year, I started going to a YMCA teen fitness class for a while but I didn't like it. The class was fine and they had you do good stuff but it was the other kids that were annoying. There were nine of us and because we were all teens it was like we all suddenly infected each other with the *I'm too cool for this* disease. The instructor, Brenna, was nice and she had a good routine but it was just too annoying with everyone acting like jerks.

Life-in-STYLE! class is totally different. There are about ten regulars and a few others each week and they are all grown-ups and they are all serious. They want it. And when I'm there, I end up wanting it too.

Like Craig, who's in his forties and a doctor. "There's the young Jedi," he says to me as we head up the stairs to the workout room. He's wearing his usual workout shirt that has a picture of Yoda and says THERE IS NO TRY.

"Hi, Craig," I say.

"How's school?" he asks. "You surviving?"

"Barely."

Craig and I enter the classroom. The floor is shiny wood and one wall is all mirrors and then two of the other walls are lined with windows. Outside, the world is blurry with fog but in here it's warm and bright. We walk around the edge of the room collecting the gear that we will use for class: a set of dumbbells, a straight bar, a mat, a plastic step, and then a rubber half-ball called a BOSU.

"Hey," says Craig, "I downloaded those albums you told me about for Peter." Peter is Craig's son and he's in sixth grade. Craig asked me what some good albums were that Peter might like for his birthday and I told him SilentNoize and the Zombie Janitors but then also the Breakups. "He just kinda looked at me funny," says Craig, "but now I notice that he's got the SilentNoize on all the time. So thanks."

"Sure," I say.

We stake out spots on the floor and arrange our gear so it's ready to go.

"Hi, Anthony," says Morgan, the woman beside me. She's pretty seriously overweight and wears these two knee braces and has to modify a lot of the workout moves. I think she's younger than my mom from the way she talks about things but it's hard to tell from how she looks. She tries really hard in class and you can tell it hurts. "So, do you have a review of *Virtuality* for me?"

Morgan is cool too because she always wants to know my opinions about movies. She knows I will have seen any big movie worth seeing or at least heard the verdict.

"Pretty good," I say, because I saw that movie last Saturday. "The effects are great so definitely see it in three-D. The plot is kinda what you'd expect, but Marni Kane gets to kill lots of zombie avatars, which is cool." I tell her this because I know Morgan likes movies to have women in them who do more than just scream a lot and get tied up until they get rescued by guys.

"Nice," says Morgan. "Sounds like I'll have to go tonight."

"Yeah," I say, and it's cool how these adults don't treat me like some kind of problem or burden or failure and how they think I have interesting things to say and like I'm an expert on music and movies. It's so different than school and home. If this was how all adults acted, things would be so much better.

Instructor Mike walks in, wearing his black T-shirt and workout pants. He has ridiculous muscles but not too big. You can tell he earned them through years of sick workouts. "All right, let's fire it up," he says, and everybody quiets down and gets ready. We all love Mike because he is like a drill sergeant and he makes us feel like we are a unit and we can take the high ground on the battlefield against our bodies. You just know he really wants everybody to do well. Also, he plays classic workout music like Rage Against the Machine and stuff that gets you going.

He turns on the sound system now and it's nice and loud. We run our laps around the perimeter of the room, then circle up for stretching. Some of them are easy but then there are others that are tough because they're about balance.

"Remember to activate your core," says Sergeant Mike as we do those quad stretches where you pull one leg up. With him everything is about core conditioning and how your abs and lower back and glutes are like the power center of your body. We do this one stretch where we stand on one foot and then have to bend forward and put the other leg straight behind us, with one arm out to the side and the other down to touch our toes and you really have to lock your core not to fall over. It's a tough one and Craig kind of fudges it and Morgan and I both go for it and end up wobbling and having to put our other foot down a lot, but we look at each other with red faces and smile.

Next we do planks, which are ice-hot pain, then some work with the dumbbells and then lunges onto the BOSU. You lay the BOSU on its flat plastic side, the blue rubber half-ball facing up, then you squat and jump and you have to land on that squishy surface like a giant mushroom in some alien forest and stick the landing. It is all about activating your quads and your core, of course. These are superhard and when you watch Mike do them it is *sick* because he squats so far down and then has this huge vertical leap and *bam!* comes down on the BOSU and his entire body freezes like a concrete statue and he lets out this huge deep breath and is poised there like a ninja. I am able to stick one or two of the landings without having to step off but even then my legs feel like they're made of rubber.

After those, Mike walks around the room giving everyone a fist bump and a "Nice work," and it is forty-five more minutes of this and it hurts but we are soldiers and we can take it.

What Happened Last Night

Somewhere in the middle of the workout, as we are doing jumps and crossovers on the step, my mind drifts off and I start to hear the song again. I think about how awesome it was coming up with that, and also I think about the ending with the f-bombs, and how it's crazy but also how that was exactly how I felt and there is something amazing about that. But then I think about how those words would be a **Situation** if adults heard them. And more than anything what I want is to perform the song at Arts Night.

It bothers me how SilentNoize or a hundred other bands can play to thousands of people with lyrics way worse than what I wrote and it's totally fine because they are artists and they are telling it like it is. I know that won't be the case for the Rusty Soles. The stalag guards will never allow it. So I'll have to figure out how to change them, but I'll worry about it later because writing them was awesome and I'm still kinda impressed with myself that I even did that, and that's all I want to think about right now: how I'm a songwriter and also rocking these crossover steps samurai-style.

Radio Silence

Class knocks me out but it feels good. Everyone seems happy it's over but also satisfied. I feel like I'll be sore, and Sergeant Mike is always telling us that we can do this stuff at home during the week to keep our muscles engaged, but I don't really get to it very often. Still, I improve a little each week, land one or two more BOSU jumps or do a few more mountain climbers or crunches, and that's how you win the war, step by step, hill by hill.

After lunch, which includes me telling my parents that the wish list assignment is almost done even though I haven't touched it, I go upstairs and load up *Liberation Force*. I log on and search for Keenan but he's not online. I check my phone to see if he's texted back from last night but he hasn't. It's weird for Keenan to go radio-silent for this long. Maybe he got in trouble or something. It's starting to bother me not to know what he thought of the song, and also about what happened at Vera and if he saw Valerie.

The more time goes by, the more I get a little nervous. Maybe he thought the song was stupid. And he'd better not show it to Skye or he's *dead*.

I send him another message: *whats up with u?*

Then I get back to *LF* where I am on Level 19 and it's the Battle of the Bulge, December 1944, and we are trying to cut off the German supply lines in the snow and cold and the afternoon goes by. I play until dark, but I don't hear from Keenan.

After dinner, there's still no word. I think about getting out Merle and working on the song some more, maybe finding some high notes to record as a second guitar track that could kind of float in space above the main riff, but I don't. I'm tapped out or something. It's like there's no music left in me.

Instead I sit on the couch while Erica is watching that same princess movie again.

I have my notebook and *Feed* with me, and after a while I actually read the chapter to see how it works, and then do the stupid wish list.

Definitive List of Things I Want to Do (For Real)

1. Go to New York City with Keenan and our band. We will be in a basement club with the concrete walls painted red and there won't be a stage except for the cracked cement floor that's rubbery with old gum and stains. The lights will be on us and we will be rocking, and I won't be

off to the side just playing guitar while someone else sings—it will be me in the middle. And I will be under one of those blue kinds of spotlights they always use just for the singer, and it will feel like the most natural thing ever. We will slam the chords to the Flying Aces section, and I will scream out my words as sweat drips down my face, the guitar wailing, my voice warped and spun and folded by the cool effects that the soundman with the tattooed arms and like thirty piercings will be adding, and the crowd will be in a frenzy, pumping their fists to the rebel refrain, and it will be everything and all and now.

2. Own a Lamborghini. (I wasn't kidding, Ms. Rosaz.)

3. Can we go to Antarctica? Like on a converted Soviet icebreaker, and see the ice and the southern stars and then set up and shoot a music video there, like a whole thing about a yeti? And when the skeptical director points out that the yeti is actually from Nepal, we will explain that, duh, we know. The backstory of our vision is that a yeti was brought to the South Pole by the Nazis as part of a secret supersoldier testing program, and in the video, Keenan will play the part of a ruthless doctor, and Valerie will be the prison guard who takes pity on me, and of course in the end we'll save

the yeti too. And also have a killer snowboard chase sequence.

4. Complete a half triathlon, where you run and swim and bike but not as much as a real triathlon where you end up crapping on yourself.

5. Eat a muffin without counting.

Armistice Day

"Here," I say, and show my mom, but I don't stick around for her to act like she won. Bottom line: at least it's done.

Later, she comes up to my room and hands back the notebook. "This is really good," she says. "I'm glad you did that."

This seems to put an official end to yesterday's battle, and I note, silently this time, that my dad's earlier threat of taking away *extra activities* has still not been cashed in. So Arts Night is still on.

"Yeah" is all I say to respond. But then Mom doesn't leave. She stands there for another minute. I hear her sniffle. "What?" I ask.

She shakes her head. "You're just so grown-up, that's all. Those dreams in your list . . . the band, the muffin . . ." She sniffs again. "They're just very different from when you were little and you wanted to take a vacation to the moon."

I don't like to hear Mom cry. The sound fills me with the same nervous worry it has since I can remember. And yet I almost tell her that I don't feel grown-up. And what is it with parents being sad about us growing up? It was their idea to have us. They knew what would happen.

"I didn't realize you wanted to run a triathlon," she adds.

"Mom, it's just a list."

"I know." She nods, then wipes at her face. "Okay. Good night, kiddo."

"See ya."

I have an urge, like we should hug or something, like that would be good and when was the last time that happened? But I don't move and she leaves and closes the door.

I sit there for a minute, wondering how I'm supposed to deal with sad Mom and angry Mom. Does she love me or is she disappointed in me?

I grab my phone and look for a response from Keenan. Still nothing.

I can't believe the whole day has gone by without a reply. Maybe he hates it. If he does, that will make it easier to change the lyrics. But wouldn't he be wrong? It was good, wasn't it? Enough time has passed since I made the recording that I'm starting to doubt. And I don't want to listen to it again, because what if I've been completely wrong about it this whole time? I wish I had some feedback.

I send yet another text—*Report in, soldier!!*—and then Dad offers to take me to the new James Bond movie, so I go.

The movie is pretty good, especially the chase scenes and gadgets. And there's a girl who's super hot and obviously a double agent. But afterward Keenan still hasn't responded.

9 DAYS

The Crowd Groans

It's Sunday afternoon and I am hanging out watching football just after the early game is over and the Seahawks have stomped another hapless foe on the road. The late games haven't started yet so it's highlights (which is kind of the best part anyway), when Keenan finally calls.

"Hey," he says in his mumbly Keenan way.

"Where have you been?" I ask him, and what I am dying to know is if he heard the song and if he liked it or what but then he is saying:

"Me and Skye broke up."

Whoa.

"You did?" I ask. "What happened?"

"She was really mad about that whole Vera thing," says Keenan, "because she wanted us to go to Red Robin with Meron and Katie. Then when you bailed, I said we could do her plan but then it was too late for some reason and she just went with them and I ended up doing nothing and then when she texted me yesterday morning, she said we were too different."

"That's it?" I ask.

"I guess," says Keenan. "She says I always choose my friends over hers."

"Yeah, but I'm your bandmate. It's different."

Keenan just sighs. "And I guess last Tuesday, I got annoyed at her chewing gum while we were watching a movie. I don't know, I don't even remember."

"Huh." Keenan sounds actually depressed. I've never really heard him this way. "So she broke up with you over *text*?"

"Yeah, but shut up, you got dumped in a drink line."

"True."

For a second I imagine a big crowd watching a Jumbotron and groaning because Keenan and Skye were some kind of record. And really, even though they were super-annoying to be around as a third wheel, they also seemed to like being with each other and sometimes you felt like there was a Hollywood sound track around them or something, like they would stick together in high school and go to the same college and all that stuff.

But whatever. Right now I know what a friend is supposed to do, and that's say, "Well, forget about her. She's annoying anyway. You're better off without her. Just think of all the girls we'll meet at shows."

"Yeah," says Keenan halfheartedly.

"Plus she always has all these opinions all the time and it's impossible to deal with."

"Yeah," Keenan says again.

"Also," I say, "she's got a big nose," except that's barely true and I don't really totally believe the other stuff either but right now I'm just trying to help.

"Ha," says Keenan. Finally he perks up. "So . . ."

"What?"

He makes a little chuckling sound. Suddenly he's all mischievous.

"What?" I ask. "The Hawks? The running game could have been better but a win is a win."

"You're funny," says Keenan. Now he sounds like he is grinning big.

"What?!"

"Come on," says Keenan. "The *song*."

One Hundred and Forty-Three New Comments

"Huh?" I say.

"Wait . . . you really don't know?"

"Don't know . . . what?"

"Did you ignore the hundred emails from BandSpace?"

I've been on and off my email all weekend and haven't really gotten anything. "What are you talking about?"

"Okay . . . ," he says, kinda laughing like he thinks I'm joking. "Seriously?"

I am starting to get nervous. "What emails from Band-Space?" I ask.

"About the song!" says Keenan. "Comments and plays and downloads. You haven't been getting those?"

"No." I am starting to decode at least some of what he is talking about. I set up the BandSpace page to send emails to our Rusty Soles email account but then never set up forwarding to my normal account. I used to check the band account a ton back in the spring and summer, but then we barely got any messages anymore and checking it was depressing and so I basically forgot about it. "What are the comments about?"

Keenan makes a big exhaling sound. "You need to see for yourself."

"Okay, fine." I start upstairs to look on my computer. "What happened?" I ask Keenan. "Did somebody find 'Star People' and like it?" I can't imagine why people would suddenly be finding our song from last year's Spring Arts Night. It hasn't gotten a single play or download since August.

"I'm not saying anything," says Keenan.

I get upstairs and I am feeling really nervous all of a sudden. We always hoped that more people would discover "Star People." (By the way, that's Sadie's title, *not* mine.) I guess it's cool if people have now. Better late than never.

I log into the Rusty Soles account, and . . .

Whoa.

There are all these messages in the inbox that either begin with "New Comment on Your BandSpace Profile!" or "Check it: A fan downloaded your music!"

"No way," I mumble to Keenan. I start to scroll down and . . . this is crazy. The whole first page of the inbox is full and that's *fifty messages*, all from the last day and a half. I click Next and see the second page of the inbox and there are fifty more messages. I click again. Forty-three more. That's 143 messages. I click on the first one. It's a "comment" about the song and the comment reads:

2:07pm 11/15: Maya42 says:
Yeah!!!! love it!!! :)

Okay . . .

But then I notice the first line of the email:

New Comment About Breakout!

"Hey," I say, "what is 'Breakout'?" but the nerve fireworks are going off inside.

Maybe I already know the answer.

Out There

"Your new tune," Keenan says. "The one you sent Friday night."

Keenan's words hit my chest like ordnance going off. It's like back in *LF* Level 17 when you're sleeping in the pub where Greta, the hot German barmaid, let you hide out as you make your way toward Allied lines, and you wake up to the sound of an air raid beginning all around you. Sound seems to get pushed beyond an invisible wall, and there is just smoke and the ringing in your ears.

Suddenly my throat is tight. "Whoa," I say. "Wait. You put that *up?*"

"Yeah," says Keenan, "'cause it rocked! And also because I was mad at Skye and feeling crappy about all that, trapped, you know, just like you sang about."

"But it was just a demo. . . ."

"I know, but I put some bass on it and it sounded kinda great. So, I uploaded it Friday night and I meant to tell you but then I've been dealing with the breakup all weekend, but I figured you'd get all the emails anyway so it would be this awesome surprise. I can't believe you didn't know until now!"

"You put up the tune. . . ." I am tapping like crazy, getting myself to the BandSpace page for the Rusty Soles and then there it is, "Breakout," a second song at the top of our music player.

The song autoloads and so I am just staring at it like an idiot and it starts to play and there's the quarter-note kick drum and the Killer G riff and *no way*, that's me singing and it sounds even crazier as a low-quality MP3 through the tiny computer speakers and I immediately want to sing it over, better, but also I cannot believe this because now I am understanding what exactly this means and what exactly I did and what Keenan did and now I am seeing the three numbers that are listed beside the song:

"Holy crap!" I shout into the phone.

Two thousand three hundred and eighty-four plays.

"I know, right?" Keenan says, and he sounds like he is psyched despite the breakup and I think I am psyched too but I can't tell because it's like everything inside just got five notches too tight.

"I gotta go," I say, and hang up.

This is insane.

Um . . .

TWO THOUSAND THREE HUNDRED AND EIGHTY-FOUR PLAYS!!!!!!!!!!!!!!

Fans

I try to remind myself of the things you read online: how some of the plays are inadvertent and so the number of people who actually listen is less than the number you see but there are only like three hundred kids in our entire school so where are all these listeners coming from?

Below the player is the string of comments and you can only see the first six:

2:04pm 11/15: chilliningreenwood says:
hella cool :) that is SICK!

2:01pm 11/15: rockluvr says:
F*** this place tru peoplz!!

1:17pm 11/15: echo says:
best song evr! Email me EvyRain61@chicamail.com gtg >:0

12:58pm 11/15: revolucion says:
F*** yeah song is mad tight you ROCK!

12:47pm 11/15: tomhenderson says:
sucks

11:35am 11/15: gabi says:
rusty soles kick a**!!!!!

As I am looking at them a little bubble pops up saying "New Comment!"

I refresh the page and look at the plays and now it says 2,395.

Eleven plays in like a minute.

The new comment says:

2:12pm 11/15: kisa says:

hi from Philippines all my bffs LOVE this when r u touring?

I stare at the screen.

I stare some more at the screen.

I am staring at the screen and then I refresh again.

Plays: 2,402

I wait a few seconds and click again.

Plays: 2,405

OMG!!

Again.

Plays: 2,417

We Are World-Famous!!!!

I cannot believe this.

I scroll through more of the comments. There are the usual jerks—and I've been one of them, who post a mean comment just to do it because the point of the Internet is that you *can*—but it's only like three or four and the rest are freaking out and excited and saying how much they love the tune and that's *my* tune they are talking about.

I find six comments that seem to be from girls and give contact info like Comment 38:

4:55am 11/15: vampkitty says:
You're the only one who understands text me 510-555-0713

And then other things like Comment 29:

11:38pm 11/14: peasncarrots says:
the rusty soles have fans across the pond! The UK sez hello and we luv u!

The UK. We're basically the Beatles.
Or Comment 6:

6:17pm 11/14: mikedog says:
sister sent to me this is exactly how it feels everyday thank u

There are cold beads of sweat dripping down my armpits and I can't believe this, I absolutely cannot believe this. I call Keenan back and we freak out some more, reading comments to each other, talking about touring England, what new guitars we'd buy, what kind of sweet entertainment system our tour bus should have, and on and on. And then I keep read-ing, refreshing, and when I look up the plays have risen up to 2,609, and outside it is dark.

What Are They Thinking?

All I do is read comments and refresh the playlist until it's time for dinner.

Heading downstairs, I consider telling my family because this is amazing, but then what if they freak out about the swears and want me to take it down or something? Because that is *not* an option. For the moment I think staying quiet is the best idea so that's what I do.

Then I spend the rest of the night watching the numbers and reading the comments and texting with Keenan about how our band is *famous* and we wonder if record labels are going to call or if this means something or nothing but either way we are blown away and one thing I write to him is: *This is what it must feel like!* and what I mean is what it must feel like to have your band blow up and to be a real musician. It must feel like this every day, and if that is the case, then that is unbelievable.

I think about what I wrote on my wish list last night and here it is and it's not a wish, it's actually happening, right now. And I have this weird sensation, like there are kids looking at computer screens not just from our school but all over the world and listening to this song and who are they? Who do they think I am? They probably imagine me as some chiseled little boy-band hipster with emo hair, not as just me.

But no, I don't need to worry about what they picture because *just me* is who wrote the song. So what if they're a little surprised when they see me *on tour in Europe!* It won't matter, and besides, famous musicians can work out every day and drink fruit smoothies and hire personal chefs to put flaxseed in all their meals and *whoa.*

This is all totally happening.

And then I wonder if Valerie is out there somewhere, a friend sending her the link to the song, and I wonder what she thinks. And does she dream about things like New York too? Does she also picture the club having concrete walls or does she imagine it a little more pro, like maybe with a drum riser and velvet curtains over the walls? I think about sending her a message. I don't have her number but I know where she is on the social media sites (maybe now and then I've looked at what photos she's posting). I haven't friended her yet, though, because, I don't know, what if that feels stalkery? Which is funny because it takes no thought at all to follow someone who you are *not* into in the way that I am maybe into Valerie.

But it's okay. I can play it cool. I'll see her tomorrow, and for now there is just being here with this happening.

Actually, I won't just see Valerie tomorrow. It will be everyone. All my classmates, and what will that be like now that *this* is happening? I feel a burst of nervous energy. Excitement, or worry? I can't tell.

Better to just watch the numbers.

I refresh the page again.

And again . . .

And again.

8 DAYS

The Celebrity Life

There is some kind of feeling like I have never had before when I wake up on Monday morning and I am instantly awake and my heart is racing. I check the stats on BandSpace while I'm still lying in bed.

Comments: 63

Downloads: 114

Plays: 2,721

Those numbers didn't go up as fast overnight as they had during Sunday and I am maybe disappointed by that, but whatever. It is pouring rain outside and so Dad gives me a ride to school and I eat my blueberry flaxseed muffin (just like my personal chef will want me to eat) on the way.

As we are pulling into the school parking lot, my guts start to do backflips and I feel a little queasy: how many kids will know? And what will they think? What if it just so happens that those few kids who made jerky comments online are actually all my classmates, because Seattle can be kind of a picky music town, and what if I'm an outcast? But no that's stupid.

I need to relax.

When I get out of the car it happens to be mostly little kids around. They're clueless, so I settle down a bit. Big breath. No problem.

Inside, though, the middle school wing feels crowded and I have to fight the urge to look around at everyone and see who is staring at me or pointing or snickering or not even noticing or what.

I tell myself to act like rock stars do. When SilentNoize arrives at a show, they walk right past the press and Jake Diamond has his silver-rimmed mirror sunglasses on and he keeps his head perfectly straight like he doesn't notice a thing.

That's what I try to do. Because also, maybe it will just be business as usual.

But then I see Blake and Natty from my class and they are looking at me and they are laughing. I immediately worry that they think the song is dumb but then when they catch me looking, Blake makes the devil horns with his hand, index and pinkie fingers up, the international sign of rock. "Yeah, Anthony!" he says.

This makes a bunch of other kids look up and that includes some seventh graders and also a few eighth graders and it happens all around me and it's like I can't tell who is looking at me like they *know* and who isn't. And even Blake's grin is hard to read: is he serious or sarcastic? What if he isn't even talking about the song? But of course he is. Ugh! It's like my brain has split into two voices that are shouting at me at the same time and one is saying, *He didn't mean it he hates it,* and the other is saying, *He loves it you are a rock star!*

I feel like basically I have no idea. Does Jake Diamond ever wonder these things? Probably not. He always seems *sure*.

So I just keep walking, hoping I look like I'm taking it in stride, and when I get to my locker Keenan is there and that's when I see that he looks completely different.

He's wearing a black Kneebacks T-shirt with a glittery skull design on it, and he's put some kind of junk in his hair and the front is sticking up and it's so different from his normal shaggy mop. He falls against the side of the locker beside me.

"Hey," he says, and then gazes up and down the hall at the passing kids, a smirk on his face. "Tons of people know."

"Cool," I say, trying to match his tone even though my insides are still flipping around like a fish on a dock.

"Almost three thousand plays." Keenan says this just a little bit louder and I look up at him kinda like *What is with you?* But then I see that he is looking over my shoulder and when I turn, there is Skye at her locker with Katie and Meron and as soon as their alien female radar picks up on me looking in their direction, the three of them immediately throw their heads together like they are some kind of three-headed hydra and they are all whispers and giggles and I turn away fast because there is nothing you can do when the evil females ignite their uni-brain. But then I notice that Keenan is still staring at them, and looking maybe a little hurt. As of Friday he had that uni-brain with Skye but now his transmission has been cut.

I punch his shoulder. "Hey," I say, "forget about her. She's missing out on a rock star, remember?" This makes us both grin and Keenan manages to nod a little. I realize that Keenan's new outfit is probably to make Skye jealous.

"I never liked her that much anyway," he says, and that is maybe the biggest lie ever but I let it go and we turn to head to class.

"Hey, Anthony." Suddenly the three girls are standing right in front of us, and Skye is smiling big.

At me.

She's holding her books in front of her in this innocent pose like she just stepped out of a movie from the 1950s. Her hair is down and it looks more styled than usual. Plus she's got more makeup on than normal. I have to say, she really looks hot, and that must be terrible for Keenan. I glance over and he's kind of frozen in the headlights. This is bad, and I'm not sure what to do. Should I act friendly like I usually would? It was one thing to say mean things about her to Keenan, since I was trying to help him get over being dumped, but I don't feel like I can be mean to her now. We're friends, well, and exes too, but . . .

And yet then I am also wondering: did she hear the song? And if she heard it, what did she think? And, man, she looks really cute.

All of these thoughts have me just standing there again, and I realize that I need to say something, and I just mumble,

"Hey," and hope it sounds friendly enough for Skye and cold enough for Keenan.

"We all think the song is *amazing*," says Skye, and when she says it she is definitely just looking at *me* and it is like *uh-oh*. I find myself thinking about swimming with her at Magnuson Park last summer. She looked hot in her bathing suit. And she didn't care how I looked in mine.

"It's really good," Meron adds, and then, as if things weren't confusing enough, I see that Meron is aiming a similar kind of innocent dreamy look *at Keenan*. Skye doesn't seem to mind this. Behind them Katie is checking her phone, bored.

And I notice Keenan noticing this look from Meron and this makes him brush at his special new hair and that does hook a quick glare from Skye but then she tosses *her* special new hair and gazes back at me.

This is insane.

"I've probably listened to it like a hundred times already," says Skye.

"Thanks," I say.

"So good," says Meron. She looks pretty hot today too, with her hair in these cool braids.

"Thanks," Keenan mumbles.

"I mean," Skye goes on, "your song . . . it's like you knew *just* how I felt. How everyone feels." And she is oh-so-very-evil because she reaches out and does that girl thing where she touches my arm to make her point and I feel her fingers and then the sharp edges of her newly purple-glittered fingernails. "It's really deep."

Keenan definitely notices this.

And I am just standing there trying to figure out what to do about this and thinking *Oh no* but also thinking *Sweet* but then *Oh no!* again.

"It's really deep," Meron says again to poor Keenan, and then she does the touching *his* arm thing and that snaps him out of a trance where he was maybe staring sadly at Skye.

The bell rings. Finally.

"Oh," says Skye. She rummages in her bag, and out come two new buttons. These are two inches across, and it's just one big picture of Winky's head, but then with a mustache drawn above his beak and a red velvet smoking jacket pasted below his neck. There's a quote bubble beside his head that says, "Well, hello."

"Would you guys mind wearing these?" Skye asks, and she hands one to Meron to hand to Keenan, and before we can answer she leans in and starts pinning the other to my sweatshirt. She is close as she does this, her leg touching mine for a second, her elbows against my chest as she puts the pin in. And I can smell that same coconut conditioner she still uses in her hair, and it's weird because I feel like I am back at Magnuson Park, two places at once, and the feeling is sort of slippery like I might time-travel or something.

She presses the pin through and then pats the button. "Perfect." She looks up at me and because I am now an infinite time traveler, I am suddenly forgetting the current reality and just thinking that she is very cute, and kind of right in front of me, and does she want to see the bombing of Dresden by airship? I could take her hand and we could run out the back door to where my TARDIS is parked.

"Come on." Katie pulls on Skye's shoulder.

"See you later," Skye says.

"Yeah," I reply, surprised it doesn't come out in a British accent, and all of that is totally insane because I think the Doctor is corny anyway and how can all these thoughts be caused by a random hair-product smell?

I shake my head and turn to Keenan. He's standing there, eyes on the floor, looking sort of spaced out or sad or something.

"Sorry," I say weakly, "I didn't know what to say. That wasn't cool."

I figure that we are about to head into bad territory because his two-day ex-girlfriend who is my previous ex-girlfriend was maybe (definitely) just hitting on me and for a second I was kind of (definitely) into it and even though girl drama makes us even *more* like a real band, this is also exactly the kind of thing that usually kills bands.

Keenan finally looks up. "I think Meron likes me." He looks shell-shocked but also happy. "She said the song was cool." He checks his new hair again. "I always kinda thought she was hot."

"Oh, yeah, she was totally into you," I say, and leave it at that. We head to science, where Mr. Scher spends the whole class droning on about how the slow and boring plates of the Earth move in slow and boring ways except for when something cool like an earthquake or a tsunami happens.

But I'm not listening. My thoughts are spinning. I'm glad that Keenan doesn't seem mad at me, but Skye acting like she's into me again . . . And how much have I tried all fall not to think about how much I liked her? And then there's Valerie, who I'd been thinking about possibly girlfriend-wise up until a minute ago. But is she ever thinking about me?

Skye is.

Still, even though Keenan played it cool, he'd freak if I got back with her, wouldn't he? And would I even want that?

Then I remind myself that I should be thinking about the song! Not all this business. The song that I never even meant to show anyone, that is now changing everything.

Lost in the Fog of War

I've been looking for Valerie in the halls all morning, but I haven't run into her. We don't sit near each other in any classes, so I haven't had a chance to ask about her weekend and also see what she thought of our song. I figure she's heard it, since it seems like basically everyone has. Like near the end of social studies, when my table-mate Mica, who is one of the weirder kids in our class, leans over to me. He is superskinny and wears bright purple jeans and usually just T-shirts even when it's freezing. He looks like an anime artist drew him. Most of his hair is dyed midnight blue and it hangs down over the whole left side of his face and then he has a big line of white in it. He wears tons of those bracelets that are just black and made of rubber.

"Anthony," he says to me, and even though he said my name, it still takes me a second to realize he's talking to me. We only really speak when Ms. Connell makes us read sections of our textbook to one another so she doesn't have to do anything. "A friend of mine in PDX sent me a link to this song by the Rusty Soles. That's your band, isn't it?"

"Yeah?" I say, and it comes out like a question because I'm trying to catch up with what he's talking about and then I remember that PDX is the airport code for Portland, Oregon. For some reason, people sometimes call the actual city that, the same way they call Seattle "Seatown."

Mica looks at me like he's impressed, though it's hard to tell for sure because I can only see half his face, and maybe that other eye is glaring or missing or cyborg, but then he says, "I was really surprised." He starts nodding to himself and he looks away but I hear him whisper-singing, "F*** this place, I gotta break out, f*** this place . . . ," as Ms. Connell goes on.

I am left wondering if that was really a compliment or actually some kind of sarcasm, but given everything that's already happened this morning I figure all the evidence seems to point to people meaning what they say and maybe everyone really does like the song and maybe I am actually now some kind of rock star. And for the twentieth time today I am blown away by a feeling that is basically: *whoa!*

Then after class, when Keenan and I are walking to math, we see Ms. Rosaz and Mr. Travis standing outside of the classroom and they both glance at us and there is something about that look that makes me suddenly think that they know too. Could they have heard the song? How would they even know about it? And if they have, what do they think? They'd have to disapprove, wouldn't they?

But they don't say anything as we pass by and they just keep talking about their weekend. I hear Mr. Travis desperately trying to woo Rosaz with his stories about studying for the National Boards (it's totally obvious to all us kids that he's completely in love with her), and yet I can almost feel their eyes on my back as we continue down the hall.

Finally, I find Valerie outside math class. She has this red sweater on with giant pink snowflakes that are so bright I almost have to squint. It's cute. Hair in two braids. Also cute. Kind of a big zit issue on her chin that she hasn't covered up to a professional degree like some of the Pockets would (or Skye today), but who cares?

We arrive at the door at the same time, so Keenan drops back as I say hi.

"Hi," she replies, but doesn't really look at me.

I keep walking beside her but it feels weird now, so I ask, "Did you hear the song?"

Valerie looks like she has no idea what I'm talking about. "What?"

"The song," I say, "online."

She cocks her head at me. "Whose song?"

"Oh, um . . ." I try to hide my disappointment: is she really one of the only kids who didn't hear it? "Just, I worked on the Killer G tune."

"Oh."

"Yeah, some new lyrics, and I sang them and then we put it up online and it's been a big hit. It's gotten like thousands of plays."

Valerie nods and says, "Wow, that's really cool," but she doesn't sound like she really thinks it is. "You guys are like a famous band," she says, and heads across the room toward her seat.

"Well . . . ," I start, because it's not *you guys*. She's part of the band. And why is she acting this way—

But then suddenly *duh*, it hits me. If Keenan never went to Vera on Friday, then Valerie never got the word that I got in trouble. She probably thinks that, at best, we just bailed without bothering to tell her or, worse, that I didn't want to hang out with her. I can't believe I didn't think of that! I just thought it was taken care of, and then the song happened . . . crap.

I hurry over to her as she's unpacking her bag and sitting down at her table. "Hey, I got in big trouble on Friday night. I wanted to come to Vera but my parents wouldn't let me out because of an email home from Rosaz. And I told Keenan to tell you but then he and Skye were breaking up, so he never made it there either. . . ."

Valerie listens, like she's wondering whether to believe me. But when she looks up she sorta smiles and I know that

I barely saved the day. "Oh, that sucks. I was looking around for you."

"Sorry," I say. "I really wanted to be there. And I didn't even know you didn't get the message until yesterday and then I thought about dropping you a line but we're not friends online anywhere."

Valerie does a little nod and I realize now that maybe all weekend, when I was thinking about us being in a band in New York together, she was thinking that I had just forgotten about her. Oops. *Idiot!* Well, but anyway things seem to be better now, so I ask her, "How was the show?"

Now Valerie finally smiles for real in that squinty way. "Oh, it was amazing. Lost Puppy was great and everybody loved Fractured Senses but to me the Clones were the best." She keeps talking and she's speeding up as she does. "Their stuff was really great and they had an amazing drummer. He had this beat for their last song that was like paradiddles on the toms—oh." She suddenly stops and glances at me nervously.

"What?"

"Sorry, that's a geeky drum term. That probably sounded pretty dumb."

"No, what's a paradiddle?" I ask, and I do mean it that it's not dumb because what Valerie doesn't realize is that a girl using geeky language about anything like video games or skateboarding but especially music is actually the *opposite* of dumb. It's one thing for a girl to be hot. It's another thing for her to talk about paradiddles.

"Oh, well." Valerie looks around a little self-consciously. "A paradiddle is right-left-right-right, then left-right-left-left." As she says it she moves two of her books beside each other and then starts drumming with her hands (which are kind of big and look a little dry and don't have any nail polish). She does sixteenth-note alternating like she describes, starting slow and then getting really fast.

"Nice," I say, and I picture some drummer dude doing that on his toms at Vera and think it's cool that Valerie thought that was cool and I wish I'd been there to see that with her. Then I imagine her doing this in the New York club and the soundman is making the lights blink at the same speed and that makes the crowd flicker and seem like a horde of zombies and the scene gets crazy.

"Well, maybe they'll play around town again," I say, and what I mean is that maybe we could try to set up another date sometime.

"Sure," she says, "that would be cool," and because Valerie isn't a Pocket she doesn't make some coy smile or anything, she just kind of nods like she is still thinking it over but I'm pretty sure she means it. "I'll check out the song during lunch," she says.

"Cool," I say, and then add quickly, "there's a drum track on it but it's just a stupid programmed loop."

"It's not your other drummer?" she says.

"No—no, there's no . . . ," I stammer, but then she smiles and I realize she was just messing with me.

"Okay," says Mr. Travis from the front of the room, "let's get started."

"See you later," I mumble, and then retreat to my table feeling scrambled and definitely not making eye contact with Keenan, who I can feel grinning at me from across the room.

But I'm barely in my seat when I hear Mr. Travis say, "Anthony, Valerie, Keenan . . ."

We all look up and I get this big earthquake inside like my abdomen has become the Ring of Fire or something (yeah, Mr. Scher, I heard that part of class) and the tectonic plates are sliding around against one another.

I suddenly feel certain Mr. Travis is going to say something about the song. But even if he's heard it, there's nothing he can say. School can't touch what we do on BandSpace. And besides, I don't need to feel like I've done something wrong by writing those lyrics. I haven't done anything different than any other *real* band or artist out there, and all the plays and comments prove that. Still, my pulse is racing.

"Mr. Darren wants to see you at lunch," Mr. Travis says, and then turns away and maybe that was totally normal.

I glance over at Keenan and he nods at me with a big grin like he knows what's up. Wait . . . has Mr. Darren heard the song? Suddenly I'm nervous in a totally different way.

The Real Test

After math the three of us head across school. On our way, a girl I don't know who's maybe in the sixth grade shouts, "Rusty Soles!" and she and her pack of friends all smile and laugh.

One of the others says, "Woo!"

Their eyes stay on us as we pass.

"What was that all about?" asks Valerie.

"The song," says Keenan. "You've gotta hear it."

"Oh. We're not in trouble with Mr. Darren, are we?" Valerie sounds nervous.

"No way," says Keenan, and again he's talking in his new, slightly louder voice. "I emailed Mr. Darren the song yesterday and told him how we had something for Arts Night."

"You did?" I try not to sound nervous and I try to stop feeling nervous but I still do. "Well, what did he say?"

Keenan smiles. "He said cool and he'd check it out with us today. Like right now."

"So you knew this was coming?" I ask him.

"Yep," he says with a smile.

"Anthony, does it have the lyrics you showed me at Jupiter on Friday?" Valerie asks.

"Yeah," I say.

"Cool," says Valerie. "Those were great. I can't wait to hear it."

"Thanks," I say, but I have a hard time smiling with the storm of nervousness inside.

As we step into the lounge I'm practically shaking. The

verdict from Mr. Darren *and* Valerie. Right now. And I realize that all those hours I spent reading comments and watching the play numbers yesterday were fine and all, but this, right here, is the real test. The two people, other than Keenan, who I want to impress the most.

Mr. Darren is sitting on one of the folding chairs with his tablet. "The Rusty Soles," he says, tapping the screen. "Come on in."

We gather around him and I see that he has our Band-Space page open.

"Two thousand nine hundred and twenty," says Keenan proudly, reading the number of plays.

"That's just since Friday?" Valerie asks. "Wow."

"Yeah," I say. Still nervous.

"So, Anthony, you went singer-songwriter, I hear," says Mr. Darren. He looks up at me with his usual friendly face. "I didn't have a chance to listen to the tune yet, but Mr. Jones here tells me it's pretty great."

"I guess," I say, quieter than I mean to, more again like I'm nervous, and I'm mad at myself because I should be confident! Fearless! But I'm breathing fast and feeling sweaty.

"All right," says Mr. Darren. He plugs an audio cable into the tablet, then runs the line over to the PA and plugs in the red and white RCA ends. There is a pop as he makes the connection. He sits back down. "This one?" he asks, pointing to "Breakout."

"Yeah," says Keenan.

"Okay, here we go." He taps it. The song buffers for a second, then starts.

Even though the music is coming out of the speakers beside us we are all staring at the player on the screen, watching the little bar slide left to right over the jagged-mountain shape of the audio waves.

When my raspy voice comes in, Mr. Darren nods slightly. "Nice melody," he says, and I think, *Yes!* So far so good.

"That's you?" Valerie asks.

"Yeah," I say, and find her looking at me with a sort of inquisitive expression, not exactly awe but still it's something. Like she's seeing me different.

Except then she says, "Were you sick?"

Keenan cracks up.

"Um, no, just, I was trying not to let my parents hear me so I was under the covers."

But then I can't believe I just said that and sure enough Valerie looks at me like I'm a psycho. "You made this under your covers?"

"Well, sorta," I say.

"You need privacy when you're playing with your mic," Keenan says with a huge grin.

"Shut up."

But Valerie smiles.

The song moves on to the second and third verses over Killer G. "Interesting form," says Mr. Darren. Again there is that little nod. Each one gives me a surge of relief but also makes me more nervous for what's to come. "Good lyrics, Anthony," he adds. "Very honest. It feels true, which isn't easy."

"Thanks," I say. More relief. "They just kinda happened."

"Well, sometimes that's the best way."

The song moves into the Flying Aces section and now the countdown is on. "Cool," says Mr. Darren as the new section begins and the melody picks up. "Such a good change," he adds, nodding some more. Valerie starts to nod to the beat too. Keenan plays air bass.

But I don't. Here comes the end. I shift from foot to foot and realize that I'm holding my breath and my pulse is racing and I have this urge to reach out and click Stop before it's too late—

And then it happens.

My strange self from just three days ago, who sounds to me like some kind of alien or maybe an Allied pilot in his Grumman Wildcat radioing from somewhere beyond the Bermuda Triangle, lets loose and the three f-bombs tear over the song.

And then it's over.

The speakers hiss silence.

Nobody says anything.

Mr. Darren Goes Obi-Wan

I glance over at Valerie but she is still looking down at the computer even though the play bar has frozen in place. I watch Mr. Darren's brow crinkle. He's still looking at the screen too. What are they thinking? Why aren't they saying anything?

I can't believe how much I'm freaking out and now I feel like I never should have written that stupid song and I never should have sent it to stupid Keenan. I'm mad at myself and at Keenan for posting it and all those crazy dreams seem so ridiculous now.

After five seconds where breathing seems hard, I finally say, "Yeah, so I guess I know what you're going to say."

Then Mr. Darren finally looks up at me. It's a new expression: one part Mom-trying-to-read-me, but then one part Obi-Wan, like wondering if I'm ready to learn the ways of the Force and leave this stupid desert planet. He reaches up and rubs his chin. "About what?" he asks.

"About the end," I say.

He looks at me like he's curious. "What about the end?"

What does he mean, *What about the end?* I feel more unsteady than ever. "The f-bombs."

Mr. Darren nods. "Well, yeah," he says. "Those happened. And there are things I could say. But what do *you* think about them? Clearly they're on your mind."

Of course they're on my mind! I feel like I have no idea but then I say, "Real bands get to do it." But I immediately hate how that sounds like I'm whining.

Mr. Darren stands up. "Well, Anthony, every word a song-writer chooses should be for a purpose. Do you feel like you had purpose? Or did you write those lyrics just for the shock value?"

"No, I . . ." I have to think about that. It takes me a second and I try to think back to Friday night and to remember how I was feeling and I am getting so worked up at this point that my palms are clammy and my toes are tingling but then I realize that no, really no, I didn't use the f-word just to use the f-word. In fact, as it was happening, I didn't think about the fact that I was swearing at all. "I was just really angry," I say. "And frustrated. I'd just gotten grounded and couldn't go to Vera"—I flash a glance at Valerie as I say this—"and everything sucked and it just kinda poured out."

Mr. Darren nods. "Well, so do you feel like the lyrics at the end of the song adequately reflect the emotion that you were trying to get across?"

I think for a second and then nod. "Yeah." I point to the screen, meaning the song. "That was how it felt."

"And *that* word was the most accurate way to sum up the emotions you were feeling."

"Yeah."

"'F***' was the best word," Mr. Darren says.

It's weird to hear him say it, like it's just another word in the dictionary. Car, toaster, f***. It makes the unsteady feeling in my head get worse.

"Well, I . . . I mean, I didn't think about it like that, it just . . ." I am stammering like an idiot and a voice in my head is screaming, *Fraud!* but no . . . "It was what I felt," I say, "like I was trapped and all I wanted to do was escape from everything and, like, I think any other word didn't feel like *enough*."

"Are you going to make him change the lyrics?" asks Keenan.

Mr. Darren shakes his head and his tone actually gets a little frustrated. "That's not what this is about," he says. "Well, not yet, anyway. Look, I'd be a hypocrite if I taught you about rock and roll or any kind of music, really, and then asked you to censor it.

"I think what you're tapping into is an important feeling," he continues, "of being trapped by powers that aren't always in your control. There are a couple human responses to that, but the anger that you've expressed is certainly one of them. And to be completely honest, when I heard the end, I have to say I thought it really worked."

Yes! I feel relief like I am falling into a pool. "Okay," I say, but what I am thinking is, *Unbelievable!!* Mr. Darren likes it. The song is right. I was right. My real emotions matter and the song works! My guts start to untangle.

"But," says Mr. Darren, "I *only* think it works if what you just said is true. That you wrote those lyrics because they were the best way to express the emotion and sentiment that you truly felt, that you truly wanted to share with an audience. I mean, that's the question an artist has to ask himself."

"I did," I say, though really I didn't think about the

audience at all when I did it. But is the feeling true? Definitely! And also *Yes!* again, because Mr. Darren just maybe called me an *artist*.

But he's still looking at me like he's a detective. "And you weren't doing it for laughs or shock value."

"I wasn't," I say, and I really do feel as sure as I can be that I wasn't. "I didn't even mean to show it to anyone. Keenan's the one who put it up on BandSpace."

"'Cause it was so good," says Keenan.

"And I didn't even know about it until yesterday," I say, "and now it's this huge thing and we're getting comments from, like, the Philippines." I look at Valerie when I say this too, because I want her to know that, and I'm hoping she'll look like, *Wow!* except actually she's sort of gazing off into space, her face kinda blank. She hasn't said what she thinks yet. . . .

But then Mr. Darren is saying, "There's part of the Rusty Soles' *Behind the Music*, that's for sure," and he and Keenan and I smile.

"So, we can do it for Arts Night?" Keenan asks.

Mr. Darren's smile fades. "Okay, so in spite of everything I just said, this is the tricky part."

A Mission Against All Odds

"I hate to say it," says Mr. Darren, "but we're going to have to ask Ms. Tiernan and the faculty."

"What?" I say. "Why?"

"That's not fair!" says Keenan, because he can already see like I can that asking *them* is going to equal a big fat *absolutely not* in about a second and a half. Keenan adds, "I know bands who are underage who play at Vera who have swears in their—"

"Yeah, but, Keenan, that's the difference," says Mr. Darren, and his tone gets a little sharper. "Arts Night isn't Vera. It's a school function, with a school audience of parents and teachers and younger siblings and grandparents."

"What about Sister's Secret?" says Keenan. "We saw them once and they were at the high school and they totally swore in like every song."

"Again," says Mr. Darren, "that's high school. There's going to be a little more freedom there for artistic expression, though I bet they had to clear it too. But for middle school—"

"We're still treated like we're just dumb little kids who can't handle it," I say, and I feel all that frustration that made the whole song happen in the first place returning.

Trapped.

No options.

Stalag.

"Hey," says Mr. Darren, and he sounds a little frustrated now too, and I swear I catch a glimpse of that exhausted adult look creeping back into his face. "If you go onstage next week and play this song just like it is now without the school and parents knowing it's coming, you are definitely going to get suspended, and likely get kicked out of Rock Band altogether, so there goes the Spring Arts Night too. Not only that, since I knew about this song and didn't say anything, I could get fired, and I really like this job. I really like you guys."

He thinks for a second. "Listen, I'll set up a meeting with the faculty, and I'll be there with you and we can see what they say. I believe Anthony's reasons for writing this song, and I think it's worth explaining to Ms. Tiernan, but it runs up against a school rule, so that's what we have to do."

I hear what he's saying, and yet I can't help feeling like we have no chance. "Why don't you just say no right now? That would be easier."

"Because I think it deserves more than just a no," says Mr. Darren. "I think it matters that you tried to capture a true feeling. At your age, I think it's important to try to figure out the best way to express what you feel. I'd honestly like to have you perform this, and see what that feels like . . . but it's not up to me."

"But you know they'll say no," says Keenan, and he's sulking now. "Every kid in school loves the song but they're still going to say no."

"Probably," says Mr. Darren, "but you never know for sure. I'll set up the meeting and we'll see. Just be ready to talk about the song and what it means to you and the honest feelings that led you to write it. If anything's going to change their minds, that's what it will be."

"Okay." I nod, and I think it sounds like a hopeless battle and we are going to be the Germans at Stalingrad, and there will be too many Russians, millions swarming over us across the frozen fields, and that *sucks*. It sucks that after all that's happened with the song and the plays and the reactions from around the world and now even Mr. Darren believing in me that in the end it's not going to matter and we're going to be slaughtered.

"Don't look so down, Anthony," says Mr. Darren. "We can try. Though it's not too late to go write a nice little song about love or cars or something." He smiles at me.

"Lamborghini love," Keenan jokes.

I try to smile but it's fake. I risk another glance at Valerie, but she is still staring into space. It is killing me not to know what she thinks, and I'm fearing the worst.

"Okay, go get some lunch," says Mr. Darren. "I'll let you know when the meeting is."

"Thanks." We head for the door and Keenan is beside me but not Valerie. I look back and see her moving toward the drums.

"Mr. Darren, is it cool if I stay for a few and try some stuff I saw the Clones' drummer do Friday?" she asks.

"Sure," says Mr. Darren.

Valerie glances over at me. "I'll see you guys later." She smiles but I can't help thinking it looks halfhearted.

"See ya," I say, and I wave but she just starts slapping paradiddles on the toms.

Who Gets the Credit and the Worry

The rest of Monday goes by and I can't shake the nervous feeling in my gut about that meeting. And also I want to ask Valerie what she thought of the song but I don't have a chance. She must not have liked it. She would have said something if she had.

I turn in my definitive list to Ms. Rosaz and leave class before she has a chance to look at it. Whatever she'd say, I'm not in the mood. Then school is over. As Keenan and I head outside, three little kids run up to us, probably fourth graders. They stop right in front of me. "Did you write that song 'Breakout' with the bad words?" they ask.

"Um," I say, "yeah." I glance at Keenan, and he cracks up.

"My sister says that's her favorite song," says one boy, "and that she thinks you sing hot."

This makes some kids next to us crack up. I notice Skye look up from nearby, where she's busy collecting signatures for Winky.

"Well, that's cool," I say. The kids are pushing closer to me. "Why don't you talk to him?" I say, pointing my thumb at Keenan. "He's in the band too."

"What do you play?" one of the kids asks.

"Bass," says Keenan.

They kind of blink at him for a second, then all turn back to me. "But you're the singer and the guitar player!" one says. "You're so awesome!"

"What do you know, runts?" Keenan snaps at them. "Get out of here."

They scurry off, and as we start walking toward town, I can see that Keenan is in a dark mood.

"Don't let that get to you," I say.

"Nah, it's cool," he says, but he's just staring at the ground and I'm not sure I believe him.

Since it's just the two of us, we stop at Arcane Comics, which is something like what we used to do before girls and famous songs.

We check out the latest issue of *HyperMole*, which is from Japan and about this subterranean force of moles and voles that fight hellbeasts. It's one of those comics that you don't pick up until you check to see who's around, because really by eighth grade it's kinda too babyish to be reading, but at this point we've been following *HM* for like eight years. That's over ninety issues, plus three annuals, four graphic novels, and a brief animated series (plus the even briefer live-action-feature failure that we do not talk about) and so we're pretty invested in what happens. Plus the store is basically empty at the moment except for the two owners, Zak and Alice, and they're busy behind the counter geeking out over a *Serenity* comic because they're old.

"I had like twenty people today tell me they loved the song," Keenan says.

"Me too," I say from across the aisle. "What do you think will happen at the meeting?"

Keenan just shrugs. "I don't know but I'm not gonna worry

about it until then." He passes *HyperMole* over to me so I can get in a quick flip-through.

"Mmm," I say, and I wish I felt like he does but I don't because *all* I can think about is the meeting. "I bet not only will Ms. Tiernan definitely say no, but she'll find some stupid way to punish us for this."

"How? It's not like we did anything wrong. You wrote a song." Keenan shrugs and sounds like he might be annoyed with me for worrying. "They can't do anything about it."

"Yeah, I know," I say, but I feel kind of annoyed back at him because how can he really know what it feels like? It's like those kids said outside school: I'm the one who wrote the song and did almost everything on it, so I'm allowed to be worried about what will happen.

The rest of the walk home, I can't shake this annoying nervous feeling. It's like, I can't enjoy how people are loving the song and how the band is blowing up, because the song is something I'm *responsible* for. I don't try explaining this to Keenan, because I know it sounds like the song is more mine than ours. Except it kind of is, isn't it?

And even though that means I'm going to have more people telling me I'm awesome, it also means that if Tiernan decides to try to punish us for the song, I'm the one who's going to get the worst of it.

Not in the Mood

When I get home I check BandSpace and it's:

Comments: 81

Downloads: 157

Plays: 3,039

There's a new comment:

3:38pm 11/16: TeamAgatha says:

This is what I look like hearing your song. write me back.

There's a link and when I click on it, there's this selfie mirror shot of a girl standing in the bathroom with one hand on the mirror and one holding her phone. She's in a tiny tank top and jeans and her eyes are huge and sort of look like she's crying. She's pretty hot, but I'm not sure how old she is. She might only be like a sixth grader and this is not good. This could be my sister in a couple years. . . .

That thought keeps me from sending the link to Keenan. I try to think of what to write her back, but then I get kind of freaked out. What if she sends more pictures? I can only download so much data a month and my parents would freak if they found pictures of strange girls on my phone, and so I look at the photo one more time and then delete the message.

I get my homework done with as little effort as possible. After dinner I think about practicing, but I don't feel like it. There's too much to worry about for tomorrow. I play some *LF*, but suck and get really mad. I don't want to do anything, play anything, check anything. So I end up watching cheesy sitcoms with my parents and sister, and waiting for the night to go by.

7 DAYS

Decision-Maker

On Tuesday before school it's:

Comments: 93
Downloads: 172
Plays: 3,095

While I'm eating my Kashi and blueberries I find a comment that says:

4:39am 11/17: DJSweetness says:
want to put your song on my weekly podcast here in Austin TX. Cool?

I click to reply but see that Keenan already has.
Definitely! Go for it! Keenan wrote.
It bugs me. I feel like it should have been *my* decision about letting the guy use the song, not Keenan's. Maybe I

didn't want the song on that podcast except *duh* of course I did. Keenan did the right thing and we're a band and it should be fine, but it still makes me a little annoyed. I wrote the song. I should at least have some say.

Name Change

The day is kind of a blur and I am waiting to hear from Mr. Darren and I am hoping to talk to Valerie but we don't sit near each other all morning and I can't quite find her between classes. I don't feel like talking to Keenan really either. The podcast thing is still bugging me. But we walk to lunch together because that is what we always do.

On the way, James, the guitar player from the Bespin Mining Guild, finds us in the hall.

"Hey, guys," he says, and he's kinda shuffling his feet, flicking a pick between his fingers. "I just wanted to say how much I really like 'Breakout.'" He sounds like a rookie trying to talk to the veterans. "The riffs are sick."

"Oh, cool," says Keenan. I've noticed he's always more excited when someone comments about the music. I realize that everyone's been mostly commenting on the lyrics of the song, so this is good for Keenan because it helps keep us away from the lead-singer-guitarist-gets-all-the-attention danger zone, except then I wonder: does that mean James didn't like the lyrics?

"You guys are totally going to rule Arts Night," says James.

"Yeah," says Keenan, and I see that he's standing a little taller like he's awesome.

And now I feel a flash of annoyance again. Sure, we're a band, but it's my song, not Keenan's. It's almost like he's getting cocky about something he barely had a part in. All he did was put a bass line on it. And now he's getting compliments and replying to podcasters?

As we head to lunch, James trailing along beside us like a loyal dog, I say something that's crossed my mind these last couple days:

"You know, I've been wondering if we should maybe change the band name."

Keenan looks surprised. "Huh? To what?"

"Well, I was thinking something that fits better, like how about Android Lawman. I think it has a little more . . . attitude."

"Wow, Android Lawman is cool," says James, like he'd say yes to anything I said. "Like C-3PO in a cowboy hat."

"Sure," I say.

"But I thought we liked the Rusty Soles," says Keenan.

"The Rusty Soles is totally cool," says James quickly.

"I have that album cover idea," says Keenan.

"Yeah, but still . . ." I wave my hand. "Whatever, we'll think about it," I say.

James heads off and Keenan is silent beside me. I notice he's not looking happy anymore and I think, *Good, that knocked him off his high horse*, except then I feel guilty. Ugh . . . *whatever!* Suddenly it's all too much to think about. But that annoyed feeling won't go away.

The Execution Date Is Set

We are just about to enter the cafeteria when we hear, "Hey, guys."

It's Mr. Darren. He's just arrived and is carrying his guitar case and is still wearing his beat-up leather jacket with his motorcycle helmet under his arm. "The meeting is going to be right after school today. In Ms. Tiernan's office."

"Has she heard the song?" I ask.

"No, but I told her the situation and gave her the site to find the song." He shrugs. "So I'll see you there."

Has-Beens

We head into lunch. We are the last ones in and there is no room at the table where Skye and Katie and Meron and some other kids are so we end up sitting at an empty table nearby.

Keenan has the school lunch. He starts to eat his sandwich, and it's something breaded, either fish or chicken or some strange genetic mutation of both, who honestly can tell? It has this smell like hot salt and I have a sucky sensation of just wanting that sandwich really bad. I picture the men in the secret back room, in their white lab coats, watching my dilemma on video screens and grinning and wringing their hands. *We've got him. It's only a matter of time before his defenses fail.*

My lunch is from home. Tuna salad in whole-wheat pitas. Where Keenan has potato chips, I have a nonfat yogurt, but I maybe also bought a cookie that I won't mention to my parents. I need it today because Mom's idea that a granola bar is dessert is crazy when there's so much going on, and it's only a cookie so who cares? One cookie is not going to lead to freakin' amputation and I can't worry about everything *and* that right now.

We both sit there eating quietly. There's nothing to talk about that matters until the meeting. And I can tell that Keenan is mad about my idea to rename the band.

"You don't like Android Lawman?" I ask him after a minute of silence.

He looks at his sandwich, not me. "I just thought we were all set on the Rusty Soles. That's all. I didn't know you didn't like it." He sounds disappointed.

"It's not that I don't like it." Sitting here now, I am not feeling that same frustration as before. I don't actually mind the Rusty Soles all that much. Maybe I should drop it. Everybody already knows us as that anyway, and in the end even a name like Radiohead sounds pretty dumb if you really analyze it, but it's like once you're famous it doesn't matter and any name seems perfect. "It's cool," I say. "Saw that you wrote to that DJ."

He finally looks up. "Oh, yeah. I figured that would be cool, right?"

"Yeah, totally," I say, and he's right, *duh*, of course it's cool. Except that it bothered me. But what difference does it make if Keenan writes or me? Same band. Now I am wondering why I was mad.

"Three thousand one hundred and nine plays," says Keenan, looking at his phone.

"It's slowing down a little," I say.

"We're almost has-beens," Keenan jokes.

I smile. It feels better to smile and joke than to be annoyed. I feel a big weight roll off my shoulders. Have I been totally stressed out and not realized it?

"It's like," Keenan is saying, "pretty soon we'll be drunk all the time and they'll be waking us up on the set of a reality show." He grabs himself by the hair and pulls his head off the table, then says in a fake British accent, "What's that? Don't you know who I am, why you—" then drops his head like he's passed out.

I laugh and it feels really good and I realize this is the first time that Keenan and I have just been joking around and doing our normal thing since before Sadie got suspended, Keenan and Skye broke up, the song, any of it.

"Forget what I said about changing the name," I say. And that feels like more relief. "It was just a crazy idea."

"Nah, it's okay." Keenan shrugs. "I like Android Lawman too. We should start a side project."

"Yeah, we—"

But then my phone buzzes. I pull it out of my pocket and find a text from Skye: *Showtime*.

I look over to her table and as I do, I hear a strange trebly sound.

Rock Riot in the Lunchroom

I think I know what it is the moment I hear it but it takes me a couple more seconds to accept it. Keenan has already pinpointed the source: Skye's phone is plugged into a little white portable speaker. I've always wanted one of those but never mind that. The point is, she's playing "Breakout" and it's already in the second verse.

I hear Meron say, "Turn it up," and then Skye is making it louder and now even though it's tinny, it is definitely loud enough for the tables around us to hear and there is this rush of murmuring like a wave as all these kids are getting each other's attention.

I look at Keenan and he is frowning. "You can barely hear the bass," he says, but then he seems to notice all the kids who are paying attention and he starts to smile. "Hear it for real on the Rusty Soles' BandSpace page!" he calls out in what is now officially his *famous Keenan* voice.

Everyone is listening and there are people shushing and so then even more people are listening and soon practically the whole cafeteria has gotten quiet.

Skye is smiling miles wide at me and as the song is heading right up to the end I do have a feeling like, *This is amazing!* This is my song, our song, and we're sitting here in the normal old cafeteria, just like any other day, only now it is totally different because everyone is listening to my song!

And I hear some kids say, "No way," and feel like a hundred pairs of eyes are looking at me and I have no idea what to do so I go into blank Jake Diamond face, except I can feel that, completely unlike Jake, my face is burning red and my jaw is pulsing like there's a creature trying to bust out and make me grin.

Don't do it, don't do it . . . but then I do.

We are rock stars. This place cannot contain us.

Except once again my nerves spike because here come the f-bombs and I can't help looking around the room for any teachers. That's when I see Mr. Travis peering in the direction of Skye's table like he's trying to figure out what's going on, and now he's leaving his spot where he usually just leans against the wall reading some random grown-up novel like he's trying to set a good example for us, and he's making his way slowly toward Skye's table.

But it's too late.

Here it comes. . . .

Skye cranks up the volume even more and then *bam!*

there's me shout-singing the end and it's like an earthquake upends the room and there are laughs and gasps and a new round of shushing.

And then it's over. Skye unplugs the speaker and it and her phone are out of sight when Mr. Travis arrives beside her table.

"What was that?" he asks, and everyone busts out laughing like crazy. Mr. Travis makes that face like he's a little queasy—it's the one the younger teachers make when they are on the outside of a joke and you can tell especially with Mr. Travis that he is worried that it has something to do with him. "Hey, folks," he says, trying to sound like **Your Pal**, "whatever that music was, I'm pretty sure it was not something that was appropriate to play in school, right?"

"Rusty Soles!" Natty yells from the table behind them.

"Woo!" A bunch of people cheer and of course they do it extra loud because Mr. Travis is right there. Everyone at Skye's table is still cracking up. Mr. Travis looks around like he so desperately wants to know what's going on, and then he follows the path of everyone's eyes . . . right to me and Keenan.

Only he spies us right when Keenan is being an *idiot* and standing up and fixing his new hair again and taking a bow. "Thank you, ladies and gentlemen," he says, even though Mr. Travis is looking right at us. There's more applause and laughter from all around us, but I grab his arm and try to drag him down because now Mr. Travis is putting the clues together and what he says is "All right, boys, that's enough. No more music."

"It wasn't even us!" I say, trying to cover. And besides, it wasn't our fault Skye played it.

"Either way," says Mr. Travis. He turns away, eager not to get into an argument with us eighth graders. But before he leaves, his gaze lingers on me and Keenan like he *knows*.

Keenan looks down at me pulling on his arm and says, "What? Stand up," and he tugs on my arm but I yank it away.

"No!" I hiss, and then, "Rock stars act like they're used to it," but what I am thinking is *Come on, Keenan!* This is a dangerous mission with *no* margin for error. We can't get the teachers even more against us than they already are or we'll have no chance at this afternoon's meeting!

Keenan does sit down, but he's mad. "Why are you such a downer?" he asks.

"I'm not," I say, but then I don't have anything to add to that. Maybe he's right and I should be enjoying myself more. But even though the lunchroom is still buzzing and everyone is looking at us like we are superstars, I can feel the teachers' eyes on us for the rest of the day, like we have a bull's-eye painted on us.

The Long March

By the time we get to our lockers at the end of the day, I feel like I'm going to explode. My stomach feels weird and I've had to go to the bathroom between every period.

"Ready?" Keenan says. He's lost his smile too and looks pale.

"Yeah," I say, feeling like no, definitely I am not feeling ready.

"Good luck, rock stars," says Skye from nearby.

"Okay," I say. Skye opens her mouth to say more but then Valerie appears beside us.

"Hey," she says.

"Hi," I say back. "How's it going?" And the first thing I notice is the blank, nervous look on her face like with her mouth kinda small and how she's not really looking right at me. Then I notice her awesome Fractured Senses T-shirt with a cracked-apart eyeball on it, and so I say, "Cool shirt."

"Oh, thanks," she says, and nope, she doesn't smile. She's probably nervous about the meeting too, but also, it's pretty obvious now that things have changed since she heard the song. Did she not like it? Why wouldn't she? It seems like everybody else in school does. In the world, even. Ooh, maybe she's annoyed that I used a drum machine on the track? Drummers get offended real easy by that kind of thing.

I want to ask her but right then I hear this little snapping sound and I glance sideways and see that Skye has just popped a bubble but more important than that she is watching me talking to Valerie. No, not just watching, scanning every detail of it like there should be some kind of laser light grid shooting from her robot-assassin eye.

Keenan nudges my shoulder. I see him breathing deep. "Time to go."

"Yeah," I say. Out of the corner of my eye I see Skye leaving.

Valerie checks her watch. "It's time."

So the Rusty Soles walk up the hall and it seems like every kid is looking at us, which is now the usual, and so we are all staring straight ahead like we're cool and under control. Actually it's almost getting kind of exhausting all the time having to keep up this show for the public. I feel like I can totally understand why after the third SilentNoize album, *The Tragedy of Coulds*, the band needed some time out of the limelight.

We enter the office and have to weave between lots of little slobbering kids as their parents jostle at the sign-out sheet like hyenas around a fresh kill. I am leading the way, and when I glance over at Ms. Simmons, the secretary, she eyes us like we are POWs on our way to the stalag.

We march down the narrow hall past the office, the copy room, the supply room, and the teacher bathrooms, until we get to Ms. Tiernan's open door. She's in there, behind her wide desk. She has a fish tank along one wall and a burgundy Oriental rug on the floor like she's trying to make her office feel inviting. And it does: just like a lair.

She looks up and gives us the all-business face, no wink,

then looks back to a file on her desk. "And here's Anthony and the band," she says. "Come in."

We shuffle into the room, Keenan kind of bumping into me like we're chained together. I see that there are seven chairs arranged in a circle that also includes Ms. Tiernan's desk. Six of the chairs are empty but the seventh is not, and that's when I understand what is really about to happen.

Massacre at Malmedy

Level 20 of *Liberation Force* is one of the toughest in the game. It takes place at the end of the Battle of the Bulge, and you are part of the 7th Infantry Division when suddenly German paratroopers start dropping in through a snowstorm and things get crazy. You get swept up in troop movement only to get attacked by a German division near the town of Malmedy, and next thing you know you're part of a surrender and then it's too late. Instead of putting you in a boxcar and shipping you off to another stalag that you can escape from like in Level 15, the Germans march you out into a field with about 150 others and start shooting. It was actually one of the biggest soldier massacres of the war. There's a moment before that, during the battle, where you have a chance to get away from the group, but the point is that you don't realize that the first few times you play, and so you're part of the slaughter. Of course, since it's a video game you have more lives and so you try again. No big deal.

But when you walk into the principal's office and see your *mother* sitting in one of the chairs, you can't press Reset, and you are not going to get another life to try this again. All you can think as you see the look on her face is that you are an idiot. You should have known better. Should have seen the advancing forces, should have known it was hopeless, should have gotten out of there sooner. But now it's way too late.

"Mom," I say, but I have nothing to add.

She just looks at me. Well, it's more like a glare. An exhausted glare.

"Hi, Ms. Castillo," says Keenan, using his fine-upstanding-friend voice, and that means that now he knows too that there is no escape.

"This is Valerie," I say, thinking that I should introduce her but also trying to do anything to calm the tension. "She's our new drummer."

"Hello," says Mom. She does smile at Valerie so that's something.

I sit down beside Mom but then realize I didn't have to, but it was just habit and getting up and moving now would be awkward so I stay there. Keenan and Valerie sit down too. Ms. Tiernan keeps looking at what's on her desk. We just sit there.

A minute goes by and then I hear a voice in the hallway. It's Mr. Scher talking quietly and saying, ". . . don't understand what Darren was thinking. Why didn't he just nix it from the start? This is a waste of time."

He walks in with Ms. Rosaz and Mr. Travis. They say hi to my mom because they've all met her too many times before, and they grab seats. Each of them has brought a pile of papers and starts busily working so that nobody has to make eye contact.

There is a rustle at the door and Mr. Darren hurries in. "Hey, everybody, sorry."

"Mr. Darren, could you please get the door?" Ms. Tiernan asks. He swings it shut. There are no chairs left and so he comes over and stands behind us as Ms. Tiernan begins.

"So," she says, looking at us but it feels like mainly me, "Mr. Darren asked that we have this meeting to discuss your upcoming performance at Arts Night. He explained the circumstances of the song and so I asked a few of your teachers to listen as well. I trust everyone has done so?"

Everyone nods slowly like a panel of executioners.

"I spoke with each of your parents," she says, making eye contact with Keenan, Valerie, and me, "to make them aware of the song and the situation. I also asked Mrs. Castillo to join us today since Anthony, as I understand it, you wrote this song."

"Yes," I reply, already feeling defeated.

Ms. Tiernan goes on: "As you all know, I value our Rock Band program, and I love the opportunity it gives some of our young people to express themselves outside the classroom. We're all very impressed with your songwriting ability, Anthony. And I understand that its content reflects certain current trends in music." She must mean the language. I hate how she's talking about music so clinically. *Content. Trends.* As if I planned it like a math lesson. "Obviously, the end of the song is the reason we're here. Now, Mr. Darren says that you wanted a chance to make your case."

Even though I've been thinking about this moment, I'm still a little surprised that Ms. Tiernan actually wants to hear what we have to say. Does that mean there's a chance that she's going to say yes? I feel my nerves frying at the idea of saying anything to this group. My mind is totally blank. It seems hopeless, standing here in the frozen field, but maybe if I can get the right words out, we can avoid the firing squad. I turn to Mr. Darren and he nods and so I swallow and try to get started.

"Well," I say, but I can't figure out how to continue. I can feel my mom's eyes and everyone else's on me and the first thing I want to do is point to Keenan and say, *He did it,* because I never would have ended up here if it wasn't for him posting the song. But that's stupid. I have to remember that I believe in the song, I didn't do this as a joke, and I have to think of all the fans online, and what Mr. Darren said, but it's like I can't find the right words in my head.

"Anthony," says Mr. Darren from behind me, "maybe you could explain where the lyrics came from. How they're not a stunt."

Okay, yeah, I could talk about that. "They're not," I say. "I know everybody's going to think I wrote the song as some big joke to push buttons, because I know I do that sometimes, but that's not how this happened. I . . ." But I stop again. I like what I'm saying, but what's next?

"Other indie bands have lyrics way worse," Keenan suddenly says, and I want to kill him because he sounds whiny, and besides, *That's. Not. Why.* It's more than that. I have to find a way to say it.

And the clock is ticking. "I just . . . I wrote the song when I was feeling really pissed off—sorry, angry—and like I was trapped. I keep getting in trouble with everybody and I can't do anything right and my whole life is like I'm living in a stalag or whatever."

This makes Mr. Travis kind of chuckle.

"What?" I say immediately because, great, they're already laughing at me.

"No, nothing," says Mr. Travis. "I just thought that was an interesting analogy."

"Oh, okay . . . ," I say, "but, so yeah, I feel like I could, you know, do things right if I had a chance. But there's never a chance. And it's just so frustrating to feel like you're still being treated like a kid, and like there's no way out, nothing you can do, and so really I just wrote exactly what was on my mind. I didn't think about the fact that I was using the f-word, it—it wasn't about that. I mean . . ." I think about what Mr. Darren said. "It was just the right word, you know, for the whole feeling."

Now I see that Ms. Rosaz and Mr. Travis, but not Mr. Scher of course, are looking at me like they are noticing me in some completely different way. It's not quite like the look they give to Clara or the other star students like Maddie and Emmanuel, but still.

And now everybody seems to be waiting for me to say more, so I try to keep going. "I never even planned to show anyone, but then . . . everybody really liked it." I kinda wish I hadn't said that because it feels like I'm trying to sell it, but I think the point I'm trying to make is what I say next: "I mean, that matters, right? That people really connect with the song? Like, that it's important to them."

Nobody says anything for a second.

"Well, yes," says Ms. Tiernan, "we've seen how popular the song is. Anthony, you've made some good points. I'd like to thank you for explaining yourself, and I think everyone here understands where you're coming from. This is a challenging age."

She gives me a look that is something like sympathy, and wait, is she going to agree with me? Did I just earn our freedom?

"That said," she continues . . .

I should have known better.

Firing Squad

"Bereit!" *the German general shouts across the snow-covered field.*

"The simple fact of the matter is that Arts Night is a family event attended by our entire school, with an audience ranging in age from preschool children to grandparents."

"Ziel!" *The line of troops raise their MP40 submachine guns.*

"And thus, this performance has to be appropriate for the full range of the audience. Clearly, the f-word is not. I'm afraid that's pretty cut-and-dry, and there's no way around it."

"Feuer!" *Bullets spray the crowd in slow motion, blood flying everywhere, and we drop in a heap to the mud-smeared snow.*

Piling Up the Bodies

"So we can't perform?" asks Keenan. He sounds crushed, like I feel.

"You cannot sing the f-word at Arts Night," Ms. Tiernan says. "I think that's pretty clear-cut."

"Anthony, why not just change the lyrics?" asks Mr. Travis. "I mean, I listened to the song, and really all you'd have to do is change one little word and it'd be fine."

"That would be your best bet," Ms. Tiernan agrees.

"But," I say, "it's not one little word. It's, like, the whole point of the song."

"I thought the point of the song was feeling trapped?" says Ms. Rosaz.

"Well," I say, "yeah, that's part of it, but . . ."

"Isn't there some other way to make your point?" says Ms. Tiernan.

"I don't know," I answer. I feel like I'm losing all my air, collapsing in on myself.

Ms. Tiernan sighs like we have reached the end of the

time for discussing this. "All I can say is, if you want to perform you will have to change it, at least for this one show."

She says it like we have *any* other shows, like she's giving us some kind of choice.

"But change it to what?" I ask.

"How about, 'Forget this place'?" says Ms. Rosaz, all eager, like this is her chance to be a real writer instead of an English teacher.

"Or 'I hate this place,'" says Mr. Travis.

All I can think as they're talking is that those ideas sound *so dumb*, and I am starting to feel the tightness again. Trapped. Every time you tunnel out, you end up against another concrete wall topped with barbed wire and grown-ups in the sentry posts.

And so really what's the point? Maybe I should just say forget it, or *fine*, I'll change the lyrics, whatever, because really I knew this was going to happen, didn't I? I mean, I thought about this way back on Saturday morning.

But that was before three thousand plays! The UK! All the people who felt like the song described them, who said it was just how they felt. Or what about what happened in the cafeteria today? If I change the lyrics just because *they* say so, then what about how *we* feel? How I felt? If I change it, I'll be a sellout! That would be basically the same as having your song in a commercial for Coke or a minivan.

"Anthony?" Ms. Tiernan says.

"I don't know," I mumble, and then suddenly I feel like,

you know what? Whatever, I'm lying here riddled with bullets. I should just say the truth. "You're just treating us like babies again."

"Excuse me?" Ms. Tiernan says.

"Anthony," my mom says in her warning tone.

"Well, it's true," I say. "We're fourteen years old, but you're making us express ourselves like we're in kindergarten."

"Now, come on . . . ," Mr. Scher says.

"Anthony, that is enough," says Mom.

"Actually, Anthony," Ms. Tiernan says, "I'd argue that part of assuming grown-up responsibilities is having an awareness of your audience."

"So I should lie?" I say. "You're all always telling us to be honest, to express ourselves, but you don't mean it. You only want us to say the good things, the safe things, and you want to pretend that the bad things we feel, the hard stuff, doesn't exist. You wouldn't want *the audience* to hear it. To know how we really feel."

"But the song doesn't offer a solution," says Ms. Rosaz. "What if you wrote about that same feeling, but made it hopeful? Like, when you have that trapped feeling, what can you do to make it better? That could be powerful and inspiring for your peers."

Listening to her, I hear my heart pounding. What she's saying is making me feel stupid. Why didn't I think of that?

But no! I realize why what she's saying is so completely wrong: "But I don't *know* how to make it better," I say. "This song isn't about, like, inspiration. It's about frustration. That's why people like it. They get that feeling, like sometimes there isn't a solution."

I look around the circle at all the blank faces, either looking at me, like Tiernan and my mom, looking somewhere into space, like Rosaz, Scher, and Keenan, or looking at their hands, like Valerie and Mr. Travis. I'm saying all this and everyone is just silent, like I'm speaking another language.

It's useless.

"Whatever," I mutter.

"Okay, well, Anthony," Ms. Tiernan says. Suddenly she sounds like we're just one of the twenty piles on her desk. "I think that about does it. The bottom line is, it's school policy, so that's that. And I think you already knew that. I'll trust you to talk it over with Mr. Darren and your family and decide what to do. Thanks for coming, everyone."

The other teachers start to get up and leave and you can tell they want to get out of there. Beside me, Keenan kicks his chair with his heel.

Mr. Darren pats our shoulders. "We'll talk at practice tomorrow."

"Let's go." I look up and Mom is standing beside me. I can already hear what she is going to be saying all the way home and all night and what I am thinking is exactly what I put in the song.

But I guess you can't say what you feel.

"See ya," I say to Keenan.

I look over and find Valerie gazing at me. Her eyes flash to my mom and back, and all she says is "Sorry" and then gets up to leave. I wish we could talk more.

"See you tomorrow," I say, and follow Mom out.

No Escape

Everybody knows how the car ride home goes with parents when they are mad. There's the not talking, then the loud radio, but the radio is annoying, and so there's the angry clicking off of the radio and then the silence again. Then about a mile from home, it can go one of two ways: either you get the ultimatum, or the pre-ultimatum bonding that is just a trick to make the coming ultimatum seem reasonable. But Mom surprises me by going with a third option, which is even more silence.

And that's actually another annoying power that parents have because by the time we are pulling into the driveway, I have this uncontrollable urge to apologize, to crack. But I keep reminding myself that *no*, I didn't do anything wrong!

Keenan texts me a little later: *Parents = not happy.*

I reply: *tell me about it.*

I lie low doing homework until dinner, though at least half of homework time is me checking BandSpace.

Then dinner is stupid just like you'd expect it to be.

When Mom finally talks, she says, "I wish you'd told us about this beforehand. I did not appreciate having to hear about it from Ms. Tiernan."

Oh, I feel like saying. *I'm so sorry you had to be humiliated like that. How sad for you.*

I just eat.

Mom keeps going. "I can't believe you put that song online for anyone in the world to hear."

"I didn't put it up," I say back, "Keenan did."

"Oh, and you don't have the power to pull it down?"

"Mom, people love the song! If you'd been on the site you'd see all the plays and comments, and kids at school tell me it's like this amazing thing."

"I *have* been to the site, Anthony," says Mom. "I've seen all the profanity-laced comments. You—didn't you think about how you were presenting yourself?"

"What, you mean being honest?" I shoot back, and *blammo!* that's a good one.

"There are other ways to express—"

But I cut her off. "Mom, that's how I felt! Why doesn't anybody care how I feel? And it's how other people feel too."

"Anthony," says Mom, and I see the moment of uncertainty in her eyes, like she wasn't expecting me to make such a good point. She gets quiet. "We do, we . . . we do."

I don't say anything else, because maybe I know they do care, that they do worry about me, but part of what they think shows that they care is exactly the ways they make me feel trapped. Or something. And anyway, they're parents. They couldn't possibly get the song and how it feels, the way the rest of my world does.

After a minute, Dad says, "Have you decided what you're going to do about the show?"

"No," I say, and shove a forkful of steamed broccoli in my mouth so that I can't answer when he says more. But he doesn't. Still nothing . . .

Then Mom talks with Erica about school, and then dinner is over and I get out of there.

I spend the rest of the night not wanting to think about the whole stupid day today or what I'm going to do about the song or any of it. I want to wake up tomorrow and not have this choice between sucky and more sucky. I just want to go to sleep but then I just lie there wide awake. I could play guitar, but I don't feel like it. I could play *LF,* but I don't feel like that either. Nothing sounds fun. Nothing is fun to think about. I'm lying in my bed going nowhere and the only thing that's moving is time ticking by in my stupid life.

6 DAYS

Death by Danger Twins

I shamble through Wednesday, all zombie. No shower, exhausted, bag hanging off my shoulder, and the urge to eat all the brains around me.

Nobody says anything to me about the song. Some people seem to look at me and the look is strange, like they are feeling sorry for me, and I figure word has gotten around about the meeting.

And every time I see one of *them,* the teachers, I get that feeling like they are watching me, wondering what I am going to do. Change the words? Don't play the show? I can't decide which option sucks worse.

I'm not the only one who's a zombie by Wednesday afternoon, though, because during last period we have a School Spirit Dance.

That's right, our school dances are during the school day.

I know.

I didn't realize that I could feel even more hopeless and

defeated, but being here in the school gym while a few cheap lights spin and a portable stereo blasts distorted songs by lame bands leaves me feeling pretty certain that life cannot get any worse.

Nobody's dancing, because why would you? There's daylight coming through the windows. Actually, four kids are: Parker, Maggie, Kendall, and Ricky, but they're the type of kids that don't need a dance to give them school spirit. You can tell by their crazy spinning and laughing out in the middle of the gym floor that they already have so much they are dangerously close to overdosing.

The rest of us are leaning against the walls like we're stuck to them. Some kids have paper cups of the syrupy fruit punch of death that's being served, along with cookies, in the corner. The parent chaperones are talking louder than the kids, including Ms. Tiernan, who is standing by the door and gazing out at the dance floor like if any of the younger chaperone dads were game, she'd totally go out there and get it on like some ancient MTV video from the eighties.

Keenan and I are under the basketball hoop. Skye and Meron and Katie went to the bathroom or something like two years ago. A couple boys who tried to escape the zombie-fying boredom by climbing the rock wall just got escorted out of the gym.

The Danger Twins are the current band blaring from the stereo, and they are about as bad as it gets. They are these boy-girl twins who seem really fake like they were grown in a lab. Their voices tune perfectly together, and the only thing "dangerous" about them is that even though you hate their songs, you cannot get them out of your head.

And standing there against the wall, I am hating how well I know the words to "Clone Double Date":

> I wish we both had clones
> To take on double dates
> And we could be with one another
> And my other with your other
> And everything would be twice as
> grea-eya-eya-eya-eyaeyaaaayt

This should be the sound track to a montage about the fall of the modern world, like with bombs detonating and earthquakes and tsunamis. Actually, they could just show this stupid dance.

We don't have to be here. In yet another of the teachers' brilliant ideas about how to make this event cool (here's a hint: *make it at night!!!*), you are also allowed to hang out in the library. Ooh.

> Twi-ice as grea-eya-eya-eya-eyaeyaaaayt

I've been here about ten minutes when I finally see Valerie show up. She spots me and waves, but then Lena drags her toward the snack and punch table.

"I'm going to go talk to Valerie," I tell Keenan.

"Don't let Skye see," he says.

"Whatever. I'm allowed to talk to my bandmate."

"Sure," says Keenan, like I'm taking my life in my hands. It's not like Skye and I are anything, except she's been flirty, and I guess I have too. She's definitely been possessive lately.

But I need to talk to Valerie. I need to know what she thinks about the song, about everything. I make my way along the wall toward the drink table. I don't like this corner of the gym. Not just because it's the den of the sweet sugar sirens of death, but also because it's where I got dumped last year. So there should be sinister cellos playing the closer I get.

The floor is sticky with spilled punch. I arrive and tap Valerie on the shoulder. She turns around and has to push her straight black hair back out of the way because she has it down today, which is rare. It looks good but I've noticed that she's been having to push it out of her eyes a lot and I can tell it's bugging her.

"Hey," I say.

"Hi," she replies. She's wearing a skirt and stripey tights and a yellow shirt and the colors are bright and crazy but it all works for her. I think I should tell her that she looks good, but then our vibe is weird again and we're closer to the radio now so the Danger Twins are . . . destroying . . . me. . . .

Clo—o—o-o—o—one double date!
Clo—o—o-o—o—one double date!

"Sorry you had to go through that with us yesterday," I say, leaning toward her ear and nearly shouting.

"Oh, it's okay," Valerie shouts back. She kinda grimaces at me, which gives her a big dimple on one side of her round face. "I'm sorry it didn't go your way."

"Yeah," I say. "It sucked. What did your parents say?"

"Not much. To tell you to change it. But they didn't think it was that big a deal." She says this like she thinks it is. "Have you thought about what to do?"

"Not really," I say, even though I've been thinking about it nonstop. "What do you think I should do?"

I think this is the question I really wanted to ask her.

Valerie looks at me and the dimple of sorrow gets bigger. "Well, I mean . . . don't you have to change it?"

I shrug. "Or not play."

"I really want to play," she says. "It will be my first gig ever."

Whoa. I'd never thought about that. "Right . . ." I feel like I could almost just agree that we are definitely going to change it, just on hearing this. . . .

Twi-eei-eeice as nice, when there's four
hands holdin'

But I still have to ask: "You don't like the ending, do you?"

Valerie shrugs sheepishly. "Not so much."

"Is it the f-bombs?"

"Sort of?" says Valerie. "It's kind of a gross word."

"I feel like it's not as bad as other swears," I say. "It's not, like, a slur or something. And everybody uses it, like all the time."

Valerie's brow scrunches. "Yeah, but it's kind of . . . violent? And about sex."

"But I'm not using it in the sex way."

"I know." Valerie looks really uncomfortable. Kind of like how I feel. Then she says, "But that's the definition. Actually that's the first definition, and the second definition is to ruin or damage something and that seems messed up." She rolls her eyes. "I know, I'm a nerd and looked it up."

"You're not a nerd. I just didn't . . . I don't know."

Valerie keeps going. "And like, how come when we want to get rid of something, or forget something or destroy it, we want to f*** it or screw it? Isn't that weird?"

"Yeah. Um . . ." I have no idea what to say. I feel kinda stupid because I never really thought about the word like that, except I don't think anyone else is really thinking about it that way either. And sure, it may have these meanings, but that doesn't change the fact that it is the main word we use to express exactly what I was feeling . . . Suddenly I just want to leave.

"I just used that word because it felt true," I say. "I mean, honest."

"I know," says Valerie. "It does sound honest." She bites her lip. "It's just not really my kind of thing."

And then I have this terrifying realization: just because over three thousand people have listened to "Breakout" doesn't mean that all of them have liked it. Maybe the only people who have liked it are the few people who have written comments. That's like one hundred out of three thousand. What if the other two thousand nine hundred hate it? Maybe the reason the song is getting so many listens is because people are laughing about it or angry about things like Valerie said.

But wait, no. Isn't it the opposite?

"The end is everybody's favorite part," I say.

"Yeah, well . . . ," says Valerie. "I guess I'm not everybody." She doesn't sound happy about that. "I'm sorry."

"No, you . . ." I don't know what to say.

Twi-eei-eeice as nice, when there's eight eyes gazin'

Valerie looks out across the room again. "I'll understand if you don't want to play the show."

"No, I . . . I mean, we'll change it," I hear myself saying. Because if I'm honest . . . "I don't want to not play either."

Twi-eei-eeice as nice, when there's eight feet dancin'

Valerie nods. "I hate this music," she says. She turns to Lena and says something I can't hear. Then back to me: "I think we're going to go to the library. Want to come?"

"Um." I glance back at Keenan, and see that Skye, Katie, and Meron are back. Plus it feels too weird now. "Nah."

"Okay," Valerie says. "Well, see you later."

"See ya."

I wanna double-kiss your double face, whaow!

As I walk back over I see Skye watching Valerie go. "Talking to your drummer crush?"

"No," I say, taking my position against the wall.

Skye and Meron are joking about the sad group of dancers, but I'm not listening.

How could she not like the song? And all that stuff about the f-word and sex . . . ? What the hell? But Valerie's different. . . . I try not to be upset, to tell myself, *Forget it, she's just one person.*

But I am upset.

Maybe it mattered more to me if she liked it.

And I don't know what to do now.

So we stand there and listen to the Danger Twins sing in Auto-Tuned perfection about falling in love while rock climbing in brand-name shoes, singing words I know by heart, and I watch the idiots dance and let the stupid minutes of this stupid scene tick by and basically hate everything.

Throwing Up Arms

When the dance and the school day are finally over, we all head for mochas.

"We need to not have to go to one of those dances ever again," says Skye. It's cold and sunny today and she's wearing a deep green scarf that matches her eyes. Her smile is bright and kind of a relief.

"There's going to be one every quarter," says Keenan. "We'll never make it." He tries to rub a hand through his hair but it kinda gets stuck because he's got like a bucket of putty junk in it. And today he's added skinny black jeans with this weird woven pattern on the back pockets and if I wasn't in such a bad mood, I'd totally get on him for those looking like girl jeans, but who cares, he might as well enjoy it while he can. Our glory days are almost over. We're almost has-beens and we barely even got to *be*.

As we walk, Skye brushes up close to me and her arm is against my arm and it makes me think of Valerie not liking the song ending. "So," Skye says seriously, "have you thought any more about what you're going to do?"

I don't even feel like talking, but maybe it feels good to just rant a bit. "I don't know. But, I mean, this is our only chance to play a show, shouldn't that matter most? So I'll probably just change the lyrics. Whatever, it's just a couple words and who even cares at this point? The song online will still be the same."

And we are right in the middle of the road when suddenly *ninja!* Skye is flipping down from a light pole. "No!" she snaps, and she grabs me by my sweatshirt sleeve. "Come on."

"Ow! What?" I say, but she just yanks me along across the street and right into Starbucks. Keenan, Meron, and Katie trail behind us.

Skye pushes me into one of the maroon chairs by the door. She sits on the edge of the chair directly across from me and looks at me like I am an idiot or something.

"Anthony," she says, practically yelling, "what are you talking about? The words are *everything*! You can't change them. That's why everyone loves the song. Didn't you see what happened when I played it at lunch?"

"The words are great," Katie agrees as the others sit down on the couch beside us.

"Mmm," says Meron, and then quickly turns to Keenan. "So's the bass."

Skye throws her arms up. "It makes me so mad!" she shouts, like she can't believe the injustices of the world, which is kinda funny because I'm still thinking, what are we doing in a Starbucks? Wasn't this place the target of the thrown-up arms last week?

Skye goes on. "It's so completely hypocritical for the school to not let you express yourself as an artist." She sounds like she should be on one of those cable news channels. "The words are *the point*."

"Yeah," I say, "but then isn't the f-bomb a weird word? Like how it's about sex? And kinda violent?"

"What?" Skye looks at me like I'm crazy. "That's not what you're talking about in the song."

"No, I know . . ."

Skye waves her hand like she's swatting away whatever I'm talking about. "What matters most is that you said what everyone always wants to say. How we all feel."

I nod as she says this because I agree, although it makes me feel a little weird because it's not like I *meant* to do that. Speak for everybody. I feel like if I was going to make some big statement on behalf of teens across America, I should have put more thought into it, like, really planned it out. All I did was freak out on a Friday night.

But then again there's the whole thing where you should just go with your inspiration, which I did. And so maybe that's even better than planning it. Whatever, I can't think about it more because Skye keeps going.

"It's censorship," she says. "You should sue them."

"I'm not going to sue the stupid school!" I say.

"Well then, we'll stage a protest. Or start a petition! We could make one online and—"

"I'm not starting a petition! I don't want to deal with any of that."

Skye looks at me as serious as she ever has. "You have to do something."

I don't understand why this is so important to her, but if nothing else, her serious face is super hot. "I know . . . ," I say.

When I don't add anything else, Meron asks Keenan, "Are you really going to change the words?" She's leaning on his arm now.

Keenan just looks at me. "I don't know. We want to play."

Now everyone is staring at me, and I don't know what to think. After talking to Valerie, I thought, *change them.* But after talking to Skye I'm thinking *don't . . .*

"Guh!" I do my own arm-throwing now because *duh!* Of course the last thing I want to do is bow to the evil masters, but what choice do I have? "What good is having a song and a band if we can't play?"

"But you *can't* change the words," Skye insists.

"So what am I going to do?" I am practically shouting. "Say I'm changing them and then not?"

Skye's mouth falls open and she grabs my arm. "Oh my God! That's it."

The Resistance Fighters Plot in the Café

Everyone looks at me, and I try to wrap my head around what I have just done.

But Skye does the wrapping for me, her hands whipping around like she's composing a symphony. "It's so obvious. You tell everyone you're changing the lyrics, but then on Arts Night you sing the real ones."

"Ooh," says Keenan, his face lighting up, and he looks at Meron and her face lights up too, like they just made couple-brain first contact.

"But," I start, "Mr. Darren—"

"Mr. Darren would be safe," says Keenan. He leans forward, smiling all big. "If you tell him you're going to change the words, then it won't be his fault."

"And, oh!" says Skye, her inner activist in full effect. "We'll get everybody to go to Arts Night, and we'll all be waiting, and then, when you sing the real words, we'll all sing along! Like stand up and"—she raises her fist, acting it out—

"it will be this huge moment of solidarity! And we'll all cheer and go nuts. Wait until we see the teachers' faces . . . and we can get someone to tape it too! And post it everywhere. Anthony, you'll be a hero."

I try to form a thought or words but nothing is happening. Skye is right. I'd be a hero, and I'd have sung my song, the way it was meant to be. Still . . .

"I'd definitely get suspended," I say. I turn to Keenan. "So would you, probably." I think of Valerie, but we could just *not* tell her, and then she'd be safe. "And we'll probably get kicked out of Rock Band Club."

Keenan looks at the floor, thinking. "You know what, so what?" And for the first time since yesterday, his famous-Keenan voice is back. "It would be worth it. For the music. For the people. And we'd be heroes."

"Infamous," I say.

"Legendary," Skye adds.

I like the sound of all that, except thinking about it makes my heart race and my stomach flip.

"It's perfect," says Skye again. "Anthony, this is going to be amazing."

"I can't wait," says Meron.

I want to agree. Despite the blur of my speeding pulse, I try to imagine it:

The school auditorium is no music club or anything, but they do have a decent lighting system and Mr. Darren knows how to make it look good.

The red padded seats packed with kids . . .

The Rusty Soles starting the song with Valerie hitting the kick drum . . .

Everyone waiting, a spotlight on me, starting to sing . . .

Starting to sing the song that is known around the world . . .

And then letting those words loose, those *true* words, with so much energy it distorts the mic, and all the kids going crazy and singing along, and all of *them* looking around like in a panic . . .

The concrete walls blowing apart . . .

The sunlight streaming in . . .

The inmates rushing the guard towers . . .

And also the glares and shouts of the teachers once the dust settles. And then the suspending and grounding and lecturing . . .

But *who cares* what happens afterward? So I'd be sentenced to my room . . . I could sit in there and relive that amazing night onstage over and over! Watch the viral videos on YouTube. Who cares if we can't play the Spring Arts Night? We'll just go to the Philippines to play, or at least the Vera Project. For a sold-out show because everyone in town will have heard what happened, and after that maybe even on to New York . . .

The **Consequences of My Actions** would be worth it.

And I'd be true to the song. To all the people who believe in it. And to myself.

And so I nod to my band of brothers.

"Okay," I say.

Dropping Behind Enemy Lines

That night at dinner we are halfway through our chana masala when Mom asks:

"So, did you decide?"

"Oh . . ." I shove in a bite of brown rice, then chew, then swallow. Here we go.

"I'm going to change the lyrics," I say, and the mission is officially launched, our Allied march to the Elbe. You can almost feel the relief in the room.

"What are you changing them to?" Mom asks.

"I don't know yet," I say. "I'll figure it out. We have practice tomorrow."

"Ms. Rosaz had a good suggestion, I thought," says Mom.

"Mmm," I say.

"Well, I think that's the right choice," says Dad, "and then you still get to play the show, which will be great."

"Yeah," I agree, but this whole grown-up-approval thing is still annoying and so I can't help adding, "A real musician wouldn't have to, but whatever. I just have to accept it."

I get ready for the blowback from that comment, but Mom and Dad let it slide. Everything is solved, everyone is happy, and no one suspects the truth.

5 DAYS

For Bahrain!

Thursday. BandSpace is still rocking along:

Comments: 113
Downloads: 206
Plays: 3,483

There's a new comment from someone in Bahrain. I have to map it online to figure out where that even is.

The Middle East.

Awesome!

Everybody Knows

"We're gonna hit five thousand plays by Arts Night," says Keenan at our lockers.

"Yeah." I am looking around at the passing kids, and once again I pretty much have no idea what to expect from everybody, but then I start to see that today's thing is kind of a hybrid of yesterday and the days before. People still aren't talking to me about the song like they used to, but instead of kinda ignoring me like they did yesterday, today they are doing this saying-hi-and-smiling-nodding thing. It's almost like everyone has turned into miniature Ms. Tiernans and I am the richest handsomest parent to ever walk down the halls.

"Hey, Anthony." Two eighth-grade girls, Maddie and Taylor, by our lockers. Big smiles.

"Hi, Anthony." Blake and Natty outside science class. Big nods.

"Hello, Anthony." Mica bobbing his head at our social studies table, like he's listening to our music in his mind.

This can only mean one thing, so when I see Skye at lunch, I say: "You told everyone, didn't you."

Skye grins. "Not *everyone*. Just the kids I knew could handle it. And look." She swipes at her phone, then holds it out. There's a virtual invitation on the screen.

Team Winky Presents:
Rise Up and Breakout!
What: Sing-Along!
Where: Winter Arts Night
When: The Rusty Soles Show
Are you In or are you In?

"Sixty three is more than enough to make it *insane*," says Skye. "And don't worry, I've told them all what they'll be singing, and sworn them to secrecy."

"Great," I say. I guess I should have expected something like this, with Skye involved. But it's a little weird, because when people were just psyched about the song, it was something I had already done, but now they're psyched about something I'm going to do, and so there's pressure. But I remind myself that it's pressure to be a hero, and that's a good thing, except for how it's making me feel crazy inside.

Good Soldiers Left Behind

Finally that afternoon we get to practice. It's amazing that, only a week ago, we were here and waiting for Sadie and I hadn't even come up with the Flying Aces part yet or the lyrics, that "Breakout" didn't even exist.

Mr. Darren isn't there yet, so Keenan and I start getting the loops of cable out of the blue plastic bin, setting up the PA and mics. You can't get me to clean my room or anything, but setting up and putting away music gear is totally different. It matters that it's done right.

I grab the silver mic stand from the corner and set it up on the lowest level where Sadie would usually be but then realize that it's going to be mine today. I look up at my normal spot on the high back level and wonder where I should stand. Do I come down to the front now? Or is that making some kind of statement like I'm a big shot? That could be weird. So I put the stand up at my normal spot and then a music stand beside it.

Mr. Darren walks in. He's on the phone. "Look, I'll see what I can do," he says with a sigh. "We can live without a sound check. We've played the Tractor how many times? No . . . I know you like to dial in the stage sound, it's just, Camille has this math night at school. . . ."

He notices us listening and I see that expression on his face, the tired-grown-up one. "We'll chat later." He hangs up, checks the time on his phone, and says, "Oh hey, didn't realize I was running late." Then he smiles. "Mr. White, Mr. Novoselic, nice to see you."

Normal Mr. Darren is back but I feel bad for him about that phone call. He's trapped in a stalag too, trying to play his music but having a family and even things like teaching us in the afternoons get in the way. And all that plus gigs at the Tractor on a Thursday are probably not what he dreamed about as his life in music. He mostly wears the same couple outfits every time we see him, and that's probably something to do with money. Maybe all that is why he wanted me to at least fight for the song lyrics at the meeting: because we are both artists who have to battle through so much to do what we love.

But maybe Mr. Darren and I are also different. He is on the has-been side and I am on the will-be side, or maybe I should call it the could-be side. I *could be* the singer who sings the lyrics that matter when it matters most, who goes for it no matter what the cost, who takes the big risk for the big payoff and says what's on everybody's mind.

It's like that on every level of *Liberation Force*. No matter how carefully you learn the sequence and plan your moves, there's always some moment at the end where you just have to go for it and do something crazy, some ten-step combination of moves that also needs timing and luck, and is the *only* way to victory.

Also, if I play it safe, what if the chance never comes again? Everybody's always saying to go for your dreams and not to let them slip away and isn't *this* moment exactly what they're talking about?

So, I am *not* going to sell out, I am not going to blow this chance, I am not going to end up a has-been. In Fat Class, Sergeant Mike says you can't ever give in, you have to keep fighting, and really it's all kind of the same, right? How I don't want to end up dead on the end of a German bayonet is like how I don't want to end up old and fat with the bad circulation or the heart attacks is also just like how I don't want to end up arguing with bandmates about a sound check at the Tractor on a Thursday night instead of playing a sold-out arena.

"Thanks for running the cables," Mr. Darren says, plugging in his Les Paul. "So, Anthony, first day on lead vox. You ready?"

"Yeah," I say as I get Merle out of her case.

Valerie comes in.

"There's Ms. Blackman," says Mr. Darren.

"Hey," she says, glancing around at all of us and I feel like too quickly at me.

"Hey," I say back. It feels weird. Like I wish she wasn't here.

She pulls her stick bag out of her stuffed blue backpack, adjusts the drums, and then warms up with a couple bars of "When the Levee Breaks." It sounds so awesome. And that feels weird too.

But maybe that's all because of what Mr. Darren asks next:

"So, how'd the lyric rewrite go?"

And now is the time in the mission when we leave Mr. Darren and Valerie behind.

"Good," I say. "I changed them. I've got some new words to try." I glance at Keenan to make sure he's keeping his cool, and he's tuning his bass like everything's normal. Then I look at Valerie but she's peeling a sliver of wood off her stick. I was maybe expecting a smile of approval. Maybe she feels bad now? Guilty that she had a part in me changing them. Whatever.

I put my notebook on the music stand and open to the page where I have crossed out the f-bomb lines and replaced them with Ms. Rosaz's suggestion:

Forget this place.

It's a bonus feature of the plan that I am using Ms. Rosaz's suggestion because it makes it seem like I value her opinion. Like I'm a nice little convert.

"All right, great," says Mr. Darren. "Then let's play 'Breakout.'"

The Zündapp and the Panzerschreck

I put on Merle and step to the mic. I have to fiddle with the stand to get it far enough from my guitar that I don't bump it, but then the mic has to be close enough to my mouth. I'm pretty sure mic stands are built by morons who aren't good enough to get jobs working on drum stands. They have all these twist-tight things that never really work right. Just as Mr. Darren is turning on the PA, the boom on the stupid stand slips down and the mic thumps on the top of Merle and there's this big pop through the speakers and then a whine of feedback.

"Sorry," I say.

I fix it, then try to get into a position where I can sing and play, but then my guitar cable is stuck under the base of the stand. I bend down, but Merle bangs the stand, and it's like, okay, forget it! Being the singer and guitarist sucks!

Then Mr. Darren comes over. "Just stand like you want to be, and I'll get it worked out."

"Thanks," I say, but feel bad again. I don't like him being helpful when he can't know the truth.

"Ready?" Mr. Darren asks, returning to his guitar.

I check the positioning. "Yeah."

Valerie nods and starts the kick on the quarter notes. She's learned the version from online. She adds a simple hi-hat beat to it that sounds great too.

Keenan and I start the Killer G riff quietly, setting the

mood. My heart is racing and I'm totally sweating as the measures pass and I have to get ready to sing. Here it comes. . . .

I lean into the mic.

"You always tell me what I need to do."

It comes out whispery and the tone is kinda right. Through a PA it's not as cool as through a mic at home. Maybe I need to move back a little off the mic, but thinking about this makes me immediately lose track of what my hands are doing, and the Killer G riff falls apart.

Valerie and Keenan keep it together, but I suddenly feel like I'm thrashing around blind in dark water. Where are the bars? Where does the riff come back in? Oh, sing again now!

"You always tell me how I . . ."

But my hands lose the guitar part again.

We train-wreck to a stop, a pile of derailed cars.

Crap! This whole thing feels like a terrible idea. What was I thinking? I'm not good enough to do both these things. . . .

"Don't worry, Anthony," says Mr. Darren. "Easy fix. While you're singing, just strum a G chord at the start of each bar. Keenan and I can handle the riff. We need to clear some space in the tune for the vocals anyway."

"Okay," I say. He's right. Even though I want to play the riff, that's what the lead singer would do. Just keep it simple.

"Let's try it again."

I get a little further the next time, but then we crash and start again. My body is contorted weirdly to reach the mic, which makes it harder to make the chords with my finger, and then my throat feels tight and I need to think about relaxing to sing but then also keeping up with the tempo around me and remembering what chords come next, and this is while trying to sing the words not just on the right notes but also with the right emotion to them. . . .

I feel like I'm balancing on a circus wire, or maybe on a German motorcycle, a Zündapp KS750, and I'm careening down a twisty mountain road like in Level 21 of *LF*, escaping from the Bavarian Alps, being chased by SS on bikes and in biplanes. You have to steer the bike with one hand while at the same time holding a Panzerschreck bazooka on your shoulder, the one you grabbed from your partner, the British SOE agent who is dead in the sidecar. You're trying to blow up Hitler's home there, the Berghof, based on intel that he and his top commanders were meeting there, but your cover gets blown and so then you're screaming down the valley trying to escape, and there is this moment where you have to get the Zündapp up to max speed and jump the blown-out bridge (and you have to jettison the sidecar and your dead mate to do it, which is something I had to read about online after crashing to the ravine floor like ten times and having biplanes strafe my broken body as the Mission Fail music played). Then as you make the jump you have to simultaneously fire your Panzerschreck and hit the sentry post hidden on a rocky outcropping above the far side of the chasm.

Something like that is what it's like trying to sing and play guitar at the same time.

But after about five times through, things finally start to lock in. It's like I'm able to create this space between my throat and my hands, like separate channels getting carved out in my brain, so that my hands are doing their thing and my voice is doing its thing.

When Killer G finally feels solid, we move on to Flying Aces, but then my hands and voice get mixed up again. After a couple more tries, I get them under control and then I can focus on singing, on the build to the end, to the triumphant moment . . . except today I have to fake it with Ms. Rosaz's words.

"Forget this place! I've gotta break out!"

I can't quite get myself or these fake words to a scream like I did on the recording, mainly because I'm still concentrating on the singing and playing at once, but also because without the f-bombs, the song just doesn't have that same feeling. It's disappointing, but I remember that it *will*, when we do it live.

A few more runs and the whole song starts to work, beginning to end, and I can really see how great this will be with the *real* lyrics onstage live. We are starting to sound good and like the Rusty Soles again, like blowing that sentry post and landing on the other side of the ravine in a rain of flames and rubble. *Boom!* Victory.

Living the Dream

When practice is over, Mr. Darren nods approvingly. "Well, I have to say, Anthony, that was very well done for your first attempt. I could feel you locking in."

"Yeah, good job," Keenan says, and I can tell he means it.

"Nice job, Anthony," says Valerie, and for the first time all week she smiles at me, but it's quick and then she's on her way out. I want to catch up to her but I still have to pack up and she's moving too fast.

"Anthony, I meant it," Mr. Darren says as I put Merle away. "That was good stuff today. I'm really glad you decided to change the lyrics. It would be a shame not to play the show."

"What choice did I have?" I mutter, and that's mainly to play along at this point, but I also say, "Thanks," which I mean.

"I know that meeting was tough," says Mr. Darren. "I could probably tell you that compromise is a huge part of being in a band, or anything in life, really, but I don't want to sound like I'm preaching. Still, though, sometimes it's about doing what it takes for the larger goal, and in this case, that's live playing experience. So well done. Have a good weekend."

"Thanks, you too," I say, and now I want to leave quick. Even though the plan is working to perfection, this conversation is waking up the guilty feeling inside, because even though Mr. Darren will be safe next week, what if he's really disappointed in us? That might kinda suck. "Good luck with your show tonight," I say as we're walking out.

"Oh yeah." Mr. Darren kinda laughs but his face falls a little too. "Just living the dream, you know."

On the way home I think about that last thing Mr. Darren said.

Living the dream.

"Maybe he won't be disappointed," I say to Keenan.

"But we'll get kicked out of his class," says Keenan.

"Well, that part might upset him, but I mean, maybe he'll actually be secretly proud of us for going after the dream. He probably wishes he was in our place."

"He did like the original lyrics when he heard them," says Keenan.

I like that idea better than thinking he'll be disappointed. A lot better.

4 DAYS

The Other Version of the Dream

Friday is a weird day because nothing really happens. I have this feeling all day like anticipation, but no one says anything to me about the song, though there are still lots of knowing smiles, and the play count climbs steadily on Band-Space. After school Keenan and I walk home just the two of us because Skye and Katie and Meron are raising money for Winky.

My parents don't hassle me.

Everything is fine.

So why do I feel like I'm frying inside? After dinner, I don't feel like practicing and so I just put on some SilentNoize nice and loud and get on *LF*. Keenan's not there because his aunt and uncle are over for dinner, so I replay some old levels and try to improve my kill-efficiency stats.

I'm in the middle of this when a friend request pops up on my phone.

It's Valerie. Her profile picture is her hand holding a really cool shell at the beach.

I pause *LF* and just stare at the request for a minute. This timing seems weird. I didn't talk to her today, and combined with how she feels about the song, I figured that our brief whatever-that-was where we were sort of acting like we liked each other was over. Maybe not?

I accept the request, debate whether to write anything on her page, but then decide to get back to the game.

A few minutes later, a chat pops up.

Valerie again.

Valerie: Hey!

I pause again and stare at this too. Weird. My first thought is that maybe she's changed her mind about the song. Maybe she just needed some time to get to know it better.

Anthony: Howdy.
Valerie: What are u up to?
Anthony: Not much. You?
Valerie: It's family movie night. My sister chose Super Mermaid Squad. ☹
Anthony: I'm so sorry.

I watch the screen, but there's no response. After a while I start scrolling through updates. I wonder if she's gone. Or maybe writing some sort of apology?

Valerie: So, I know about the plan.

Or not.

Anthony: Oh.
Valerie: Yeah.
Anthony: Are you mad?
Valerie: No . . .
. . .

The pause lasts like ten seconds.

Valerie: I get why you guys didn't tell me.
Anthony: It's like in spy movies where what u don't know can't hurt you.
Valerie: Ha.
. . .

Valerie: You guys will get suspended, I guess.
Anthony: Probably. But oh well.

I feel like it's sort of cool or defiant to be saying that. Also my chest feels tight.

Valerie: No more Rusty Soles, then. ☹
Anthony: I guess not really.
Valerie: We were just starting to sound good.
Anthony: We could probably play Vera, after this.
Valerie: My parents told me I can't play Vera until I'm in high school.

. . .

Valerie: This was my only shot for this year.

I want to tell her that her parents are being ridiculous.

Anthony: Oh.
Valerie: Anyway . . . I just wanted you to know that I'll keep the secret. Don't worry.
Anthony: Ok.
Valerie: Also, you sounded great yesterday. You'll be a great singer and guitarist. We
. . .

Valerie: Nevermind.
Anthony: What?
Valerie: Nothing really.
Anthony: Say it.
. . .

Valerie: Just, we could have been a really excellent band. The Rusty Soles.
. . .

Valerie: Maybe next year, or something.

I don't know what to say. I've been seeing everything that's happened with "Breakout" as being the beginning of our dream, the one that goes all the way to New York, but Valerie is making it sound like this is the *end* of the dream, or at least the end of her version. Which means she had a ver-

sion, which is cool, except that it was different, and . . . Ugh!
I can't make sense of any of this!

Valerie: I should go.
Anthony: Ok.
Valerie: See ya.

I feel stuck, like there's more I want to say. Like that I'm
sorry, but I'm not, am I?

But the screen blinks: *Valerie is offline.*

Whatever

I sit there for a minute trying to figure out what I think. I feel
mad, but I'm not sure why. I thought we'd be doing Valerie
a favor because she gets her first gig and doesn't get in trouble. But now I feel like we're taking her band away. I'd never
thought of it as her band, just as her being part of our band.

And that makes me wonder if we're doing the right thing.
But aren't we? And why should she get a say in my song?
Or is it our song?

A message pops up on my computer: *You there soldier?*

It's Keenan. I jump on and together we move on to Level
22 of *LF*. The game shifts to a movie scene explaining that our
GIs have been reassigned to help the 10th Mountain Division

push back the Axis in the Italian Alps. This is just an excuse for the game makers to design a skiing assault level, which I think doesn't make a whole lot of sense with actual history, but whatever, it's cool.

And it keeps me from thinking about Valerie. I don't know what to do with this feeling I have that I am letting her down, disappointing her. I don't feel like she should have a say, but also I do. But so many people like the song and believe in it. If she doesn't, if she thinks we should change it to please others, to be safe and boring and not offend anyone, or even because of that stuff she said about the f-word, that's her problem, isn't it?

She's a good drummer, though.

And a pretty cool person.

Different than me. Different than Skye.

I don't know what to do with it.

Ski down ravines and blow up stuff, probably, and Keenan and I are up until almost three a.m. until we finally crack the level. I wonder if it's just the action that's keeping him awake, or if his nerves are firing too.

3 DAYS

A Soldier Alone

Mom takes me to Fat Class on Saturday morning and I am glad to be locked in for an hour with Sergeant Mike and not have to think about anything else.

We do lots of weird ab work with the big bouncy exercise ball, like where you have to sit on it and get your feet off the ground so you're trying to balance on this spongy rolling thing, and then also push a dumbbell up from your stomach, legs still off the ground, until your arms are straight and it's crazy hard and we are all kind of wobbling around and falling over sideways. Morgan takes a big fall and is wincing but Craig and I help her get back on the ball.

"Thanks," she says.

"Good job, Team Anthony," Sergeant Mike barks from the other side of the room, and he is the best. "Okay, take a minute to recover."

We all kind of slide off the balls, and as we're standing up and stretching Craig says, "Tough."

I nod. "Yeah." Then I think to ask Craig about music. "Hey," I say, "is Peter still listening to SilentNoize twenty-four seven?"

"Oh," says Craig. For a second he looks away and it's a look that I might not have recognized a week ago but now I feel like, uh-oh. "Not so much. He's listening to the Breakups more these days."

"They're cool too. I've totally heard kids say that Jake Diamond can get on their nerves," I add, like everything's normal, except I can feel that it's not.

"Okay, now we're going to lie on the ball," says Sergeant Mike, "like this." He gets on top of the ball and rolls forward on it until his hands are on the floor and he's squeezing his glutes and his legs are sticking straight out. "Then you're going to do a push-up extension, like this." He starts doing push-ups with his legs straight and his abdomen on the ball and you can just tell by how his body is so rigid that this is going to be killer. We all try it and I fall off once but manage to get about five of the push-ups done.

And then we are standing again and between exhausted breaths Craig says, "Peter still likes SilentNoize, but I actually took it away from him. . . . We listened to it in the car and I, um, I guess I didn't realize the kind of language in that stuff."

I feel a cold fist form in my gut and all I can say is "Oh."

"I mean, I know I'm old," says Craig, "but it was a bit much."

"Yeah, well, Peter's still kinda young, I guess," I say, trying to sound like we're brothers on the field of battle, not like we're a grown-up and a kid because that's suddenly how I'm feeling and it's like I feel embarrassed or dumb or I don't know what.

"You know," says Craig, "I get that's what kids are listening to these days, but I just think bands like SilentNoize ought to think about their audience. Like think about what they're saying to kids, and all that. Peter's only eleven, you know? Anyway, I just don't want him listening to that kind of thing yet."

"Sure," I say, and I wonder if he thinks I'm *only* fourteen, and I wish I'd never given Craig SilentNoize. I would never play that music for my parents or teachers and now Craig is sounding like them.

"All right, one minute of cardio," says Sergeant Mike, and we all have to run laps around the perimeter of the room.

Craig starts to take off and pats me on the back. "Hey, no worries."

"Okay," I say, and I start off too, jogging around the room, breathing hard, hating jogging, but hating that whole conversation way more. I try to remind myself that it is completely okay to like SilentNoize. I didn't do anything wrong by suggesting it for Peter because *tons* of middle school kids are listening to them, but then I realize that this also means that Craig probably wouldn't like *my* song either.

And along with Valerie, that makes two.

And that sucks! I wonder again if singing those words is

the right idea, and I have to spend the rest of the day reminding myself that yes, it is. That the whole school is counting on me. That there's nothing wrong with it because the words are true. It's how I felt and it's the school rules and society that are being dumb, not me.

I mean, right?

2 DAYS

Six Blueberries in a Red Bowl

Sunday I wake up and check BandSpace:

Comments: 127
Downloads: 231
Plays: 3,656

There is also a new comment:

1:43pm 11/20: RainCityTalent says:
Hearing some great buzz about you guys! Wondering if you
need representation. You could be big!

No way!
I immediately text Keenan: MANAGEMENT!!!
AMAZING! he writes back. *I want six blueberries in a red
glass bowl and sparkling water served at 52 degrees!*

We make a couple more jokes about ridiculous tour rider requests, and this blows away the frustrated thoughts I'm still having about Craig and Valerie.

I search online for Rain City Talent and find a Facebook page. It seems like they, or he, or whoever, have one client called Gremlin Wing. I find them on BandSpace and they are a kinda okay metal band. Still . . .

Management! That's like . . . that's like the beginning of rock stardom. And so then I'm thinking who cares about what Craig and Valerie think when someone in the business, some-one who *matters*, is thinking this.

Shock Value

After watching football, I practice a bit and then it's dinner-time and it's Sunday so we are making pizza. We do a whole-wheat and flaxseed crust and nonfat cheese, then olives and turkey pepperoni and red peppers and no, it's not like restau-rant pizza, but actually it's pretty good. I like rolling out the crust. That's usually my job. I make four so that everybody gets their own personal pie to put toppings on. My crusts are pretty perfect, round and thin in the center with thick edges.

We have fun, the four of us, making our pizzas and making a mess. It's one of the few times when Mom and Dad drink wine and so they loosen up and we joke and it feels easy.

We are eating when Dad says, "Heard you practicing. How's it going?"

"Fine."

Then it's quiet for a second and he adds, "I like it."

I look at him. So does Mom. "What?" I ask.

"The song," he continues. "I like the song. Those are some good riffs, and, Anthony, you did a great job on the guitar and the melody. Your voice sounds good too."

I stare at my food and eat more quickly. Dad doesn't really ever say stuff like this. And I know since he used to sing and play in his band that he means it. It feels like I've made him proud in a real way. "Thanks," I say quietly.

"I'm glad you're changing the ending too," he adds, "because that way everybody can hear how good you are, and they won't be distracted."

"Mmm," I say, but . . . distracted? Distracted by hearing my real emotions?

Dad takes another bite and then says, "If you had done the song with the f-words, that's all anybody would remember afterward. They wouldn't remember the great guitar player, the great singer."

I look up at Dad, the former musician, and suddenly I feel like, *Whoa,* Dad just made a good point. I do picture everyone freaking out about me saying the f-word, about the shock value of that, but I didn't think that maybe it would distract them from the point of the song.

Except, no, it won't. This is just another example of adults not giving us enough credit. Everybody in *my* audience thinks the words are really good and that they matter, that they're part of the art. Grown-ups have lost that. They just see a world of rules.

But still I say "Thanks" to Dad. For the compliment part. And I mean it. It is nice to hear that he thinks I sound good.

Then I eat quickly and get out of there.

And when I am upstairs I just feel like there is all this static in my head, too much, and for the rest of the night I'm in a crappy mood, because I have no idea what to do with all these things. What Valerie said, what Craig said, but then Rain City Talent, and now what Dad said. Why does everyone have to have an opinion? Why can't the song just be what it is? It all leaves me feeling overwhelmed, like the only thing to do is *not* think about it, so I zone out and play *LF* until I can finally sleep.

1 DAY

Keenan Makes the Call

On Monday, I'm just as confused, only now it's the day before the show and I feel like there's a little motor inside me, humming along and keeping my body running faster than normal. Everything is so intense.

I try to explain it all to Keenan as we're walking to our final practice. I tell him about all the opinions: Valerie, Craig, my dad. And after that I say what I've basically been thinking all day: "I just don't know if it's worth it."

And I really don't. Having to deal with all these opinions and expectations is making me crazy. "You know," I say, "like, I know the words are *right*, and true, but . . . all these adults are going to totally freak and we're going to get in so much trouble and then we'll get kicked out of Rock Band Club and we won't have our next show, and so it's like, why bother? It's too much of a pain." I don't totally feel like that came out right but it's the best I've got at the moment.

And even just talking about it makes that little motor

seem to spin faster, like it has a dial that goes to 11, and if normal Anthony life is 3, it feels like now it's turned up to 5 and slowly rising.

We stop outside the door to the lounge. Keenan looks at the floor like he's thinking hard. He's added a black belt with square silver studs to his cool-hair-jeans-shirt appearance.

"Are you mad?" I ask him.

"It's just that you're talking about doing what's right for *them*, not what's right for *us*."

"No, I just . . ." But maybe I am. Crap! I throw up my hands. "I can't tell anymore!"

Nothing about the plan seems clear. It's almost like this plan, this song, is as much of a stalag now as everything that the song was about in the first place!

Keenan looks up and I have no idea what he's going to say, but then he puts his hand on my shoulder like he's my commanding officer or something, which is how Keenan *never* acts. "Tomorrow night is going to be awesome," he says. "Everyone's gonna be there and all we have to do is do it like we planned. It's going to be the biggest thing that's ever happened. Ever. And who cares about everything else? What's the point of having Rock Band if we're censored little babies? Tomorrow night will be our time to say what we want."

Yes. Okay. I nod and say, "Yeah," because he's right.

He's so right.

"We can do this," Keenan says. He's really ready for battle. I'm almost jealous, but then I remember that his job is easier than mine. He just has to play bass. But actually maybe he has a second job and that's dealing with me, because even though I want to just agree and shut up I still can't stop all this worrying.

"But . . ." And then I'm kinda surprised because what comes out is what my dad said. "Is it going to be the biggest thing ever because we rocked and the song was amazing, or just because everybody's going to yell the f-word at a school event?"

Keenan shrugs. "I don't know. Kinda both, I think. Right?"

"Yeah," I say, but while it's the best I've felt since sometime last week, I still feel that motor. Even Keenan's words haven't totally erased the doubt.

But what happens next does.

We walk into the lounge and there's Valerie sitting behind the drums and there's Mr. Darren sitting with his Les Paul—

And there's Ms. Tiernan sitting across from him.

"Boys," she says as we stop in the doorway, "I just dropped by for a quick chat."

Confrontation

Mr. Darren says it's all about timing.

Like when you have just been wondering if what you're about to do is the right thing, and because of girl drummers and workout partners and parents you've been starting to doubt it . . .

And then your principal says to you, "I've heard a rumor that you're thinking of singing your original lyrics tomorrow night."

"Huh?" I say.

Tiernan narrows her eyes at us. "Is this true?"

"No," I say immediately, and I go into defensive maneuvers. "I mean, kids want me to, but I changed them. Mr. Darren's heard it." I look over at Mr. Darren but he's looking down at his guitar.

"Yes, so he tells me," Ms. Tiernan goes on, peering at me like she's an intelligence officer who's going to get me to confess no matter what. "But you could be lying to him too."

"We're not!" says Keenan.

Ms. Tiernan makes a clicking sound with her teeth. "You know, I think we're going to have to cancel the Rock Band Club performances for tomorrow night."

"What?" It comes out as a shout but I can't help it.

Her reply is made of ice: "I am not going to have my students shouting the f-word at a public event."

"That's so unfair!" I say. "You're punishing us and you don't even have any proof! Not to mention ruining the night for the other two bands."

Ms. Tiernan looks straight at me for a second, and I can see her wheels turning. "Okay then, Anthony, you know the rules of this school. Give me your word I can trust you to obey those rules tomorrow night, if I let your band play. Can I trust that you won't let your band, or the other bands, down?"

I just stare at her. I want to burn her with my eyes. And I want to yell it at her all over again, how all I did was write a song about how I felt and she's *wrong* to censor it, *wrong* to make me promise not to be true to my art, to sell out, *wrong* to trap me like this, like she doesn't respect us at all! I want to tell her all of it but *I already told her*, and what good did it do? She won't listen. She never does.

So I square my shoulders and suck in my gut and nod and glare at her straight in the eye and say, "Yes."

"Keenan?"

"Yep."

"Valerie?"

Valerie studies the tips of her drumsticks, then she meets Tiernan's gaze. "Yes."

Ms. Tiernan stares at me again, a computer spinning, and I think, *Ha. Called your bluff.*

"Okay," she says. "It's my policy to believe a student who gives me his word. And I trust everyone to respect this community and its rules." She stands up. "Sorry to take up your time, Mr. Darren." She heads for the door.

"No problem," says Mr. Darren, eyes still on his fret board.

Valerie peels a sliver of wood off one of her sticks.

"Oh, and one more thing, gentlemen," Ms. Tiernan says from the doorway. "In case I didn't mention it: I'm sure you realize that there will be major consequences if you sing those lyrics onstage. Suspension, kicked out of the Rock Band for the rest of the year. And not only will you be throwing away the rest of this year with Mr. Darren and this program, there will be a note about this added to your permanent record that will stay with you through high school and beyond."

"Okay," I say, almost sounding enthusiastic. Bring it on, Mein Herr!

When she's gone, it's quiet. We get out our axes. Once we're set up, I step to the mic and Mr. Darren is looking at me and I can't help saying, "What?"

"I know why you might be thinking of doing it," says Mr. Darren.

"We're not going to!" says Keenan.

Mr. Darren shrugs. "I'm just saying, from one musician to another, I understand it." He starts to pluck at the Killer G riff. I'm expecting him to say more but he doesn't.

"We're not going to," Keenan says again, and I'm like, *Shut up, you sound guilty!*

"I heard you," says Mr. Darren, and when he looks up at us he's smiling, but it's less than usual. Tired, is how it looks. And while I've seen him make that face so many times, now he's joined the ranks who've made that face because of me. "Okay, Valerie, let's rock it."

And we do. We play and it goes well. I'm getting the hang of the motorcycle/bazooka control that is playing and singing. And it all sounds good. Good enough that I have some spare brain space to replay the conversation with Tiernan, to feel my anger rise, and to think:

I'm sorry, Mr. Darren, I know you're exhausted, and I'm glad you understand, but they *don't.*

And that's why the doubt is gone.

Tomorrow night we're busting out of the stalag once and for all.

SHOWTIME

Sound Check

I barely say a word to anyone all day Tuesday and it is like that motor in my body has been cranked up two notches and is spinning at 7 now, and so my heart rate and my breathing are too quick and then everything else around me seems to be in kind of a blur, like I'm outside of time or something. It feels like that all day, until Mom is about to drive me over to the school that night. I have to be there early for sound check, and then before we go I get completely stuck standing there in my room trying to figure out what to wear.

I feel like now I completely understand why Jake Diamond has a personal wardrobe consultant, because this is way too much to worry about. I never care much about what I'm wearing but suddenly it completely matters because there are going to be hundreds of people watching us and we are going to be rock stars and if that's not a time to make sure you look good then I don't know what is.

I try the blazer and T-shirt look: *sucks*.

T-shirt only: *sucks*.

Untucked, unbuttoned button-down over T-shirt: *sucks*.

And so in the end I leave my room with a storm of clothes all over the bed and floor, and there I am in the car wearing my same dark gray hoodie sweatshirt that I always wear and the same baggy jeans and the only thing different is a new maroon Zombie Janitors T-shirt. The top of the design, a mop handle that has a corpse head impaled on it, is just visible. I'll just be me, is the idea. Everything else looked even worse.

"You nervous?" Dad asks me on the way.

"Kinda," I say, which means *yes, so much*.

"Will you be playing with a music stand, or have you memorized the words?" Mom asks.

I can see right through this question. She wants to say something about the old words, but she's trying to tiptoe around it.

I feel like snapping at her but I have to keep my cool. "I can't have a music stand onstage," I say, like that idea is ridiculous. "But I've been practicing. I think I've got them."

I wait, wondering if Mom will push it further. "Well, just do your best," she says. "We're very proud of you."

You won't be, I think, and I don't like that thought, but still: doing what's best for me is not what's best for them. And there's no way they're going to understand that.

They drop me off and go for Thai food, saving me some for after. I find Keenan in the student lounge. His journey to the indie-rock side is complete now that he's wearing a ratty white long underwear top that hangs down from beneath an old Posies' *Frosting on the Beater* T-shirt.

We know the drill so we roll the amps down the hall and onto the stage. Their wheels rattle on the wooden floor. The chorus risers fill the middle of the stage so we put the amps to either side, plugging them in and flicking them to standby to warm up as we get our axes. I am just plugging Merle into the Marshall when a light shines on me. I look up, squinting through the bright center spotlight.

"Rusty Soles." Mr. Darren's voice echoes from the back of the arcing rows of seats, where the sound and light boards are.

I get a solid hum from the amp and then hit an E chord. The sound blasts out into the room. There is something great about sound check, about cranking it up in a huge empty room that will soon be full but right now is just yours. Keenan thumps the bass and the stage floor vibrates and that is *rock*.

The door squeaks open and Valerie shuffles in carrying the hi-hat and the snare drum on its stand. She's wearing a fancy dress, like with a high-belt waist, and it's kind of lavender and has frills that end around her knee. She's got a dark green cardigan over that. Her hair is straight with big blue barrettes on either side.

She sees me checking her out and says, "My parents thought I should dress up. I tried to kinda make it too dressed up. You know, sort of subversive." She blows at her bangs. "Not sure it worked."

"No, it totally works," I say, and try to smile as I say it because she really does look cute, and that look on a girl who

251

will then bash on the drums is pretty amazing. Seeing her makes the motor crank higher inside for what feels like a hundred reasons: being reminded that I like her, but also that she doesn't believe in what I'm about to do.

She smiles at my compliment, then puts the stands down and starts offstage. "Can you guys give me a hand with the rest?"

Keenan and I follow her and I get the floor tom, she gets the bass drum, and Keenan grabs the rack tom and the other cymbal. We are all nervous-quiet as we walk back to the stage and set her up in front of the risers.

"Guys, run a mic cable for channel one, okay?" calls Mr. Darren. "Then monitors." I loop a cable out from the direct input box on the stage floor, and then Keenan and I lug the two monitor wedges from the back and set them up at the front of the stage.

We tune and check our levels, and when Valerie has the drums all positioned Mr. Darren says, "Okay, play a few bars."

We launch into the Killer G riff and sound explodes through the empty hall. I sing a little, miss a chord and worry that I can't do it, but then settle in. I point at the ceiling to tell Mr. Darren to turn up the monitor, and we play for another minute, then stop. Our sound echoes into the dark. It's a lonely sound but an amazing feeling.

Then we clear our guitars and the Bespin Mining Guild comes out to run their song. The Random Sample never did find a replacement singer, so tonight it's just the two bands.

Keenan and I head down to watch from the seats. We sit

in the back row, just in front of the soundboard. That's where things always sound the best. I look to see if Valerie will come sit with us, but her dad arrives and they sit near the front.

While the sixth graders play, and Mr. Darren checks the different banks of lights, I slouch down in the red fabric chair, watching the way our instruments shine in the lights. Merle looks like a work of art, except for the "Merle," and yet that's cool too because it has history. I wonder what other stages she's been on. Has Merle been to New York already? Toured the world? And is she going to channel those far-off places tonight? Someday I've got to track down the original owner. I've done searches online but I've never come up with anything.

"You ready?" says Keenan.

I feel the motor inside clicking up to 8, making my fingers twitch. I'm not sure if it's just that we're performing, or what we're planning to do, or all of it combined. One thing that helps remind me why we're here is to think of Ms. Tiernan's face and her ultimatums yesterday.

"Yeah," I say. "Totally."

It Goes to 11

Parents start to arrive and the room slowly fills up. The place is half full when we hear shouting from the entryway.

"Rusty Soles!"

"Wooooo!"

We look over to see Skye, Katie, and Meron moving away from Skye's mom, who brought them, and hopping and bouncing their way over to us, all dressed up with their hair and makeup freaked out for the show. They have an *R* and *S* on each cheek.

"Rusty Soles rock!"

We've been saving them seats. Skye drops beside me and gives me a big hug. "How you feeling, rock star?"

I immediately glance in Valerie's direction, but she's not looking back here. Then I think, *Who cares if she is?* "Good," I say, trying to hide any evidence of my speeding motor, because a rock-and-roll front man should be cooler now than ever.

Each time Skye and Meron and Katie spy a group of middle-school kids arriving they shout, "Woo! Rusty Soles!" and most of the kids look over and smile back but they don't respond because they're walking in beside parents and grandparents. Mica and his emo friends are on their own, and they respond with whoops and cheers that turn a lot of heads. Also, Mica catches my eye and flashes me the devil horns. I give him a serious nod. He and his friends seem ready for the moment.

Then I see my parents and sister come in. They don't sit near me, but still I feel the motor inside kicking up to 9.

The room fills and the lights go down for the chorus. As they walk onstage, Skye leans over to me. "Everybody's ready," she says. "We're all going to jump up and sing when you do. It's going to be a rebellion."

"Nice," I say. Motor to 10. I picture POWs in drab coveralls swarming through a blown hole in a concrete wall. I picture me at the front. I swallow big.

"You probably won't even get in trouble," Skye goes on, "since it will be all of us, and they can't punish everyone." She reaches over and takes my hand. I look down to see that we are holding hands. It feels like too much. More than I can handle.

"Right," I say, but I also think about how the men leading the charge are usually the first to get gunned down.

The chorus begins. They're doing some sad piece about Christmas from like a hundred years ago. The mother sitting next to me has a program and I see that the chorus is doing five songs, and then Bespin, and then us. Two songs in, Skye leans over to me and her hair touches my cheek and she whispers, "Hey."

It's the kind of *hey* that's *important*, and so I say, "Yeah?"

"Anthony, I just want you to know, your song means a lot to me."

"You told me," I say. Motor to 10.5.

"No, like *a lot*," says Skye, and her voice gets closer to my ear and more whispery. "Listen, you can't tell anyone, but it's the reason I broke up with Keenan."

Uh-oh. "Huh?"

"I mean, I was wondering what to do anyway, but then I was awake at like two a.m. that Friday night and Keenan texted me that the song was up. He probably thought I'd hear it and it would make me like him again, but when I heard it . . . all I could think about was *you*."

255

I am trying to process this and I realize there are things I'm supposed to say right now, hundreds of movie lines, but it's not happening and then I realize I've let like three seconds go by and Skye is staring at me so I say, "Okay."

Skye stays by my ear. "You stood up for something real. You gave a voice to everyone who can't. That's so amazing. I want to do that someday, but you're doing it right now. I believe in the song. I believe in you."

My thoughts feel confused. I think about how when I came up with Flying Aces, I was thinking about wanting to change things, but then also I think about how I just wrote the song because it was how I felt. I wasn't trying to give anyone a voice. I was just feeling things. And I think about Skye and her causes, and that she's right, there are things worth fighting for. But fighting for a sparrow doesn't break any school rules. She's not going to get suspended over Winky's romantic life.

"I know you're totally focused on the show," says Skye, leaning even closer, and this time it's like she's breathing all the way into my ear, and the warm air almost makes me flinch. I start picturing those diagrams of ear canals from science class and how they connect to your throat and you have all these weird sinuses in the back of your head and stuff. "We can talk after it's over . . . ," she says, "and *more*." She touches my chest with her index finger, right on my sternum.

I feel like there is a balloon exploding in my head, making it impossible to think. I figure maybe Jake Diamond would go for the silent approach right now, so I try that too, because on the one hand, I smell Skye's coconut conditioner and maybe even for a second picture that summer sunset over the water and taste the weird sweet metal taste of Lake Washington and picture the *more* she is talking about after the show. But then I am also checking again to make sure Valerie isn't nearby.

Skye kind of huffs. "Don't you want to be with . . . me again?"

She means going out. Of course she does, and I realize I am probably an idiot for suddenly feeling like I did not see this coming, because, *duh*, Anthony! This has been coming like the Luftwaffe on a clear morning. Or maybe I did know but I've been trying to avoid dealing with it, hoping it would go away. It seems to be doing the opposite of going away. And I like Skye! Don't I? She gets this whole thing with the song. She gets me . . . I think. Ugh! I need more time to figure all this out! Why can't it wait until *after* the biggest show of my life?

And so I just try to stall: "But you just broke up with my best friend."

"I don't think that's a problem." Skye glances over to Keenan and Meron and so do I and, oh . . .

They're totally making out.

Okay, well, so much for playing the *it would hurt Keenan* card.

"Yeah . . . ," I say.

Then everyone is applauding. The chorus is finished. Which means I'm free from this moment with Skye, but also . . .

Motor to 11.

It's time.

Waiting in the Wings

Keenan pulls his face from Meron's and stands up.

"I gotta go," I say to Skye. "So, you're sure everybody is really gonna sing?" I ask, and maybe now you can even hear the motor humming in my voice. "You know where the right spot is—"

Skye cuts me off. "I know the song by heart. Everybody does. You're going to be amazing." She gives me the big serious eyes and says, "Good luck," like I'm an action hero about to break into the evil genius's lair and defuse the nuclear weapon. I nod and stand up fast before anything else can happen.

Keenan and I head backstage and we help the chorus kids move the risers. We slide the drums to the middle of the stage and roll the amps to either side and then the Bespin Mining Guild comes out.

Me and Valerie and Keenan stand behind the velvet curtains listening to Eric, James, and the rest of the band. They are rough around the edges, but I'm glad to be near their music. It gives me an excuse to not speak because the motor is running so high right now I feel like it might overload.

My hands have started to shake. I'm fiddling with a pick in my pocket and can feel the cold slick of sweat on it. I am thinking, *This is it, you can do this, this is the moment and you are going to do this*, and at the same time I am wondering if I am going to throw up or what.

And then the sixth graders are done and it's showtime.

Keenan walks by me and pats me hard on the shoulder and gives me what I guess is some kind of meaningful look. "Let's get those Nazi bastards," he says with a cowboy drawl.

I nod and want to say something back but my voice feels stuck. I catch Valerie glancing at me. "Hey," I say to her. She turns to the stage, holding her sticks with both hands and her knuckles are white and I realize again that this is her first real show ever. Her big debut. Keenan and I have been here before, but Valerie hasn't. Every second of this is new for her. "Good luck," I say. "You're going to rock."

She nods, her mouth scrunching, and then she says, "You too."

We both stand there for another second, the sixth graders shuffling past us with their gear. In this last moment, I feel like I want to say something, but I have no idea what.

Then Valerie says, "It's been fun playing with you."

"Huh?" But then I realize that she's saying this because of what will probably happen to us when it's over.

"Yeah," I say, "you too."

"It would've rocked either way," she adds, and then heads onstage.

It takes me a second to understand what she means, but then I realize she's talking about the song, about the words, and I'm filled with doubt again. Now I just want to run in the other direction because to go out on that stage means no turning back.

Standing there, with my motor revving out of control, my heart pounding, hands shaking, I wonder: what was I even thinking wanting to be the singer, writing those stupid words? Everything just feels like a mess now, but I try, I try *so hard* to tell myself, *Anthony, no, you can* do *this. This is* your *time.*

"Come on," Keenan calls from the stage.

Okay. Deep breath. Here we go.

The Rusty Soles Take the Stage

I walk out. From the distant back of the auditorium I hear Skye give a "Woo!" like I'm something special. A couple other kids do it too. That's cool.

I take Merle off the stand and sling her around my neck. The crowd was chattering but now they are quieting down. Mr. Darren lowers the houselights and the sea of murmuring faces disappears into the dark.

Mr. Darren's voice comes over the PA. "Ladies and gentlemen," he booms, "the Rusty Soles!"

Everybody cheers big.

I look out at the dark silhouettes of heads as the sound washes over me. Wow.

Yes.

And then the lights flash on. I can barely see anyone in the blinding white. I glance back at Valerie, bathed in crisscrossing blue and red, and nod at her.

She nods back, all business, and like a total pro she clicks her sticks four times.

In this last millisecond I feel a kind of sheer lightning bolt of energy, like what will happen next, what will I do can we or what I—

And then we are in.

The Moment

Now there is just music. Mr. Darren times the lights to Valerie's kick drum, pulsing on and off, and I finally feel okay. It's not just the auditorium anymore, it's the Vera Project, it's New York, the basement club like we've imagined. Here we are.

I stand with my guitar against my hip and dig into the Killer G riff. I look at Keenan and he's head down, doing the same. We're locked in with Valerie and it's tight, but I barely have a chance to enjoy it because after one time through I have to sing.

As I step toward the mic, the first verse coming at me like a wave, I think, *I am ready*—

But then I realize that I didn't remember to change the mic stand after Tyler and he's a lot shorter than me and so I have to kind of hunch over to get to it, and my lip bumps into it, and the mic gives me an electric shock as a welcome but here is the verse and there is no time. I try to control my hands on the guitar and strum the open G chord and the vocal is slipping up and out of my throat, and here we go—

"You always tell me what I need to do,
You always tell me how I need to be,
You think that I should listen to you,
When you don't care what's important to me."

And then we're through it and I survived.

Valerie's kick drum thumps. She adds in sixteenths on the toms for the second verse. Nice. Mr. Darren speeds up the lights to match. Is she playing those cool paradiddles? I want to glance back and see—

But *whoa*, I have to keep concentrating, because here comes the next verse, but already I am looking past that, toward the end of the song, like the end of a game level, coming at me.

Hundreds of people out there.

Am I really going to do this?

I know what I felt, but am I really going to shout my real lyrics into this room?

Wait, have to sing—

"You say I'm flying out of control,
You say I can't do anything right."

I'm barely keeping up but the words get out and are mostly the right notes.

My eyes flick down to the front rows of the crowd at the edge of the stage lights. It's not a crowd of Vera Project teens but instead parents, younger kids, grandparents, the exact mix that Ms. Tiernan was talking about. . . .

"But you don't know what I really can do,
And you don't want me to put up a fight."

My eyes skip away but as I'm pulling them back in I spy Mein Herr herself, leaning against the side wall, arms crossed, a few feet from the stage stairs, and I realize that Ms. Tiernan is in position for battle. If I do it, she's ready to sprint up here in her spiky heels and kill the song and apologize to the crowd. She is looking at me and I am looking at her and it is a showdown glare and *I hate her.*

Her stare says, *You gave me your word.*

Mine back says, *I will show you.*

And then the third verse arrives.

"A hundred people tell me what to d—"

But my sweaty hand slips on the neck and why is it suddenly a thousand degrees up here? And then my next chord is a half step too high and ahhh it sounds terrible—

I jerk my hand away and have to look down at the fret board. Have to get my hand back to the right fret—I've totally forgotten how to play!

Which chord—

But Keenan is still laying down the riff and I find the

chord again except then I miss the beginning of the next lyric line and barely finish it.

"... say, do what you've told."

The words jumble in my brain, skipping, I'm chasing them but they're like a truck rolling ahead of me just out of my reach. . . .

"I'm like ... inside this ... life,
... Dying when ... too old."

And we have reached the change to the Flying Aces part and I look down and say to my hand, *Please get up to* A *and make the bar chord*, and yes! Somehow it gets there.

And then we are in my part, my first songwriting ever. We are here, live onstage playing a part that came completely from me, and that's amazing and I want to enjoy it but all I can think about is what's coming, because now we are heading toward *it*, and it's like my head is crowded with a thousand voices, like everyone is shouting their opinions at me all at once and nothing is clear anymore and the universe is noise.

Mr. Darren puts a pure blue light on me. It feels like a force field beam, like I exist in some private universe.

The lead singer. Alone.

Keenan and Valerie are in greens and reds together outside it. I can barely see them.

Beyond that, in the dark space, the audience is waiting.

Waiting for me to come through. Some for me to sing my song the way it's supposed to be, to be the hero. And some for me to prove myself as either a **Fine Upstanding Student** or a **Dangerous Element**, and then some others having no idea what is coming and if they did they would probably leave or cover their children's ears.

"So I'll tell you what I wa—"

Ahh my hand slips again on the neck and I hit a C-sharp instead of the D and there is a moment of uncertainty, the universe askew as half-step notes grind against one another. I swallow the lyric and how am I supposed to play and sing and be all these things at once? And I feel like, *No*, that's it, no. I can't do this. It's too much. What were the changed words again? Forgive this place? No, that wasn't quite it and this is all too much, I never planned on this. I just wrote a song! It was never my idea to show it to the world or make a school-wide plan or

"And I'll tell you what I think . . ."

But no! I can do this! I'm not going to give up. This is my chance and what am I if I don't sing *my* song? All I am is some stupid fat kid who plays video games and who doesn't do great at school and all I've got that I'm good at and maybe even *great* at is music and everything else sucks and if I don't grab this and go for it then someday I am going to be arguing about sound checks with my bassist for two-bit shows in between hospital visits for my bad circulation when life has passed me by and *I have to do this!!!*

"And I'll tell you how I feel . . ."

I . . . but what about ruining the band? Is this seizing the moment or blowing it up?

But the end is stampeding toward me from the horizon, through the dark auditorium like the Grim Reaper on horseback. I blink at the sweat stinging my eyes and every beat that my sweaty fingers slide across the fret board is bringing us closer—

Get down to the E . . . barely, okay, got it.

Have to be in the club, in the dream—*it would've rocked either way,* Valerie said—but *no!* I'm not changing the words for *them,* this is about us, who cares about the consequences, I—

Closer . . .

I try to turn my head to see Keenan—what does he think I should do?—but there's only blue light and he's somewhere beyond that and it's up to me, alone here, and I can't see and it's time

it's time

oh God

can

can't . . .

But then suddenly I have an incredible idea.

Another Way

An idea that jumps out of the static of crazy shouting and insanity in my head.

This unbelievable idea.

I remember what Skye said: *because it will be all of us* . . . And if all the kids out there in the crowd are really going to sing . . .

Going to scream the lyrics . . .

Then what if . . .

What if *I* just don't? What if I let *them* do it?

Then we wouldn't get in any trouble. No suspensions, no getting kicked out of Rock Band Club. And Ms. Tiernan can't punish the entire middle school!

I know, I wouldn't be singing the words like I said I would, but I recorded them! The rest of the world knows the song in its true way, and I can sing it like that on the world tour with our new management!

I mean, maybe, to really bust out of the stalag, I *don't* sing them, *don't* fall into the trap, *don't* take the bait from Mein Herr because maybe that's what this is, a trap where Anthony thinks he's being the hero but really becomes the framed leader of the rebellion, the martyr, and then *they* have someone to punish, to make an example of. Maybe that's what this has been all along and I've been just about to walk right into it.

And so instead, I could get us right to the moment, all the way to the edge, and let everyone take it over from there,

like a mass of freed POWs rushing into the sun past their exhausted leader.

It will seem spontaneous, like a force of nature, rising up
from the crowd. It will be more than just me. And because it's
all of us, *they* will have to understand that these words matter,
that they *have* to be sung.

Almost there . . . My hand slides up to A. . . .

The last line is coming, and I am feeling all of this and
shaking and I sing with all the force that took me over when I
wrote it. The next line screams out of my throat.

"Are you ready to listen?"

And then here it is, okay, everybody, here's what you
wanted! I gaze at them, my crowd, my commandos out there
in the dark.

Come on, everybody!

This is it!

*Take a deep breath and get ready to take it from here! Let's
show them all!*

The moment arrives.

Now! This is it! Break out of the stalag! Here we go!

I hit the A to start the bar and open my mouth, but instead of singing, I thrust my fist to the sky just like Jake Diamond or Bono would, the international sign to sing along.

Now!

Now . . .

. . .

Distantly, from the back of the auditorium, my eye catches two silhouettes, Skye and Meron, jumping up and I hear the sharp squeal of them starting to shout, "Fu—" but then immediately it dies to nothing like a match flame being squashed between two fingers, snuffed out in the silence as they notice that . . .

No one else has jumped up.

No one else sings.

And the moment has passed.

One Second Later

My hands move to E like they are on autopilot.

Then to D.

Even as I am staring wide-eyed into the crowd.

What happened?!

But I have to jump on the next line before it's gone and my guts explode with nerves and I'm confused and my hands are like flopping fish and they lose their spots again. I look down and try to get them back in the right places but then the words too, have to sing them—

"I've gotta break out!"

It comes out garbled and then here is the next moment, the next chance. I raise my fist again . . .

269

Everyone!

Silence. Not even Skye and Meron get up this time.

Then we're past it again and I can't get the next line out at all and my fingers slide all over the fret board and everything is just noise and panic. *This plane is going down! Going down!* Have to get to the E chord . . . and somehow I barely do and then we hit the final A and that's it and I'm missing the last line again, not singing, my head thrashing around looking at the crowd, still silhouettes, then at Keenan, who's looking back at me. His eyes are wide like "Come on!" or maybe "What happened?" I can't tell.

And then the last chance has passed and that's the end, we are at the end of the song and I manage to sing the final words

"Breakout,
Into the sun . . ."

and Valerie smashes the cymbals and we hold the chord and everything vibrates and rumbles and I slam my hand against the strings

slam my hand against the strings

take it all out on the strings

so that they hear the sound they need to hear the sound

they need to hear the sound of what it felt like

need to hear it

hear it hear it hear it

and one or two more times

the sound of how it felt because I couldn't say it

and my hand is stinging and Valerie has paused and Keenan too and I look up and find them both staring at me, and though I will never know, never understand what exactly they are feeling about me right then, what I do know is that this is serious and we are a band of brothers and we have been through hell and now

it . . .

Keenan jumps, kicking his feet up behind him, and when he lands we stick the chord tight one last time. Hands on strings. Sticks crash.

is . . .

Valerie chokes the cymbals dead.

over.

No Restarts

There is applause.

It takes a second for me to actually notice that it's happening.

I don't know what to think but then the first thing I think is . . .

Oh no.

I blew it. I look out at the crowd. People are clapping. Ms. Tiernan is clapping. She meets my gaze and raises an eyebrow.

Oh no.

Mr. Darren appears on the stage and walks over to the

mic. I step out of the way. I can't look at him, just at Merle. My high E string is busted, swaying in the stage lights.

"Let's give another big hand to the Rusty Soles!" he says.

People do. There are some whooping shouts too. Most of the crowd probably just thinks I made a mistake, forgot the words, got jumbled.

We're just eighth graders, after all.

"Also," Mr. Darren says, and the crowd quiets, "I wanted to mention that most of the song you just heard was written by Mr. Anthony Castillo here." Mr. Darren glances at me and the crowd claps again. He's kind of smiling but it's maybe a stage smile. Then he turns back to the mic. "I can tell you from experience how hard it is to write your own music and perform it, and this was Anthony's very first time. I'm sure there will be many more." There is a final round of applause.

I hear it, but like from far away.

"Thanks for coming, everyone." Mr. Darren pats my back. I figure he's going to say **Good Job** or **You Did the Right Thing**, but all he says is "We'll talk." Then he jogs offstage and turns up the houselights and the crowd starts to murmur and leave.

I spin around and unplug from the amp and start rolling up my instrument cable, keeping my eyes on the floor, trying to look busy and not look out at the crowd. A minute ago feels like a year. Like I was inside some kind of bubble world and now I'm outside it and everything that seemed like it made sense doesn't anymore.

And still all I can think is *Oh no.*

What was I thinking? How could I have *not* sung the lyrics? I had my chance. I blew it. But I thought everyone was going to sing along. . . . What about everything Skye said? Why didn't they sing? Why didn't I? I was going to. It was my chance . . . and I missed it.

Did I do the right thing? I have no idea. All I know is that I don't feel right. Not at all.

My moment. My big chance . . . it's already in the past. I am never getting it back.

No restarts.

No do-overs.

Packing Up

I wrap my cable and put Merle in her case and then unplug the vocal mic. I roll that cable too, fold up the stand, and then I finally glance over my shoulder at the crowd and I'm glad to see that most everyone is gone. I roll my amp off the stage, the sound of the squeaking wheels echoing across the empty auditorium.

Back in the band room, Valerie is stacking the drums. Keenan is on the top level pushing the bass cabinet against the wall. I lug the Marshall up and do the same. Our heads are down.

"Here," I say to Keenan, holding out my hand for his power cable, because the strip is on my side.

He passes it over but doesn't look at me. He's probably

mad. He was counting on me. I had the spotlight. Our spot-light. And I failed the big mission. But I thought . . .

I don't know what I thought.

When that's done, I stand up and see Valerie's dad at the lounge door. "Hey, Val, ready?"

"Yeah," says Valerie. She starts toward the door but pauses. "Great job, you guys. I thought we were really good."

"Thanks," we both mumble. I think back and realize that despite the mess I made of the lyrics, of the chords, of the end, of everything, Keenan and Valerie both nailed it out there.

"You too," I say. Then our eyes meet and I wonder if she is glad I didn't sing the words, but she doesn't smile or anything. She just kinda shrugs and I don't know what it means. "See you tomorrow," she says, and then she leaves.

I turn to Keenan. He's standing there staring at the floor, like he does.

"I'm sorry," I say.

He doesn't say anything for a second, and then finally, "What happened?"

"I don't know." I start to unzip my sweatshirt but stop. My T-shirt is soaked and stuck to my body, a big dark stain down its front. I zip it back up.

"Why didn't you sing the words?"

"I—" I feel like I can't make eye contact with Keenan so I just stare at the floor too, then the stupid couches, the amps. And I try to explain myself. "I just started freaking out, and . . . I tried to check in with you, but I couldn't really see you. Tier-nan was right there, and then I thought that since everybody in the crowd was going to sing the words I could just let them do it. And then maybe it would be this amazing moment."

Keenan doesn't say anything.

"I wasn't . . . scared about getting in trouble," I say, and I think I mean it but I'm not sure. Maybe I was. "I just felt like, I don't know . . . It was all too much. And then there was the crowd and it wasn't, like, some cool club or anything. It wasn't New York. It was just a bunch of grandmas and kids in a stupid school auditorium and . . ." I don't know where I'm going so I stop. I'm not sure if any of that is really true. It feels like some of it is, but I barely know which parts. Then I add, "I guess I tried to have it both ways. Or something. Sorry," I say again.

Keenan is quiet for another second and then finally he kind of laughs a little to himself and shrugs. "That would have been cool."

"What?"

"If everybody sang for you. That would have been amazing. Like an uprising."

"That's what I was thinking," I say, and I'm relieved to at least hear that it makes sense to somebody else. "But then nobody did, and it ended up lame."

Keenan nods like he's made up his mind. "They were scared," he says. "Everybody's a bunch of babies. Stupid school."

"Yeah," I say, but I feel like I am too. Even just having all these worries and issues is so *not* rock and roll.

Or maybe it is. Maybe this is why singers end up at spas in Sedona. Because singing your words, expressing yourself, is hard.

But I don't think Ty from Sister's Secret would ever have this problem. Maybe that's why he's in high school and I'm still here. And at least what happened tonight didn't happen somewhere like Vera. That would have been way worse.

"You really rocked it, though," I say to Keenan.

"Yeah," says Keenan like he knows he did. "Thanks."

The door creaks open again and there are my parents. It's hard to tell what they're thinking from their blank expressions. Did they catch that I was really going to sing the words?

All Dad says is "Ready?"

I grab Merle. "See you tomorrow," I mumble to Keenan.

Keenan nods. "I'll send Rain City Talent a message," he says.

"Cool." And I am glad he's going to do that. I want nothing to do with music tonight.

I walk out into the night between my parents. Erica is next to Mom. Mist coats us.

"Great job," says Dad, like of course he's going to.

On the drive home, I expect them to ask about the ending, but maybe sometimes parents actually know when to be quiet because they don't say a word.

I stare at the lights and the rain and the dark and I remember thinking about what it would feel like to be up onstage playing my song and now I just feel like I died or something back there, and that motor that was inside me speeding up and up is shut off now and I'm hollow and empty.

Or maybe I'm just really, really tired.

Deep in the Bunker

But there's not going to be any sleeping for a while. Back home, I fire up *Liberation Force* and log in. I don't text Keenan, but then there he is online, anyway. And so together we head into Level 23, the assault on the Reichstag. I wonder what he is thinking about tonight, but luckily we don't have to talk about that.

It's the end days of the war and we're paired with Soviet fighters and have to make our way down into the underground bunkers beneath Berlin. Everybody thinks Hitler and his wife, Eva Braun, committed suicide a week earlier, but when we enter, a dying soldier tells us that no, Hitler is still alive, and of course it's up to us to take him out.

So down we go, into the tunnels and supply rooms and shattered command centers and there are booby traps and then, since *LF* has already broken with reality at this point, Keenan and I are not surprised to find zombie SS officers, which we learn are some hideous genetic supersoldier experiment gone wrong and yeah, Hitler's definitely a zombie too when we get down there and he keeps coming at us even after we've blown his head off and riddled him with bullet holes, until we finally burn him to ashes.

The Reich has fallen.

We've won.

As I learn the route through the bunker, along with the new zombie beheading moves that we need, I wonder how I could have let the moment onstage pass, how I could not have

277

come through when I had the chance. I feel like some version of me is still up there, stuck in that blue cone of spotlight, trying to figure out what to do, and will be stuck up there playing that level maybe forever.

And all I can think is that, if I really try to remember that moment, I know it was crazy, like nothing I'd ever felt before. Even though we'd practiced the song, made our plan, and even though I'd written the words and read comments from around the world, up there onstage it was still like a zombie Hitler coming at you out of nowhere. Even though you've imagined it, played twenty other levels to prepare for it, you've never had to actually do it.

And so the first time, zombie Hitler tears your guts out and eats them. And you lie there watching him slurp up your intestines and he laughs victoriously. Except in *Liberation Force*, Hitler's flesh-rotted face fades to black and the level starts over and you get to take another shot, and another, learning along the way, and eventually you win the level. You get the sequence of movements just right, and Hitler's a pile of ash.

But here, in the dark, in the almost-dawn, there is still nothing I can do to change what happened onstage. The moment looms over my broken body, digging at my insides, hour after hour. And I can't start over, can't try again.

It's just done.

143 DAYS UNTIL
SPRING ARTS NIGHT

Keeping It to Myself

I wake up and check BandSpace.

Comments: 131
Downloads: 235
Plays: 3,804

I also see that Keenan chatted with Rain City Talent.

11:43pm 11/24: RustySoles says:
Thanks! We'd love to work with u!

12:13am 11/25: RainCityTalent says:
Great, when's your next show? Assuming you guys are still in high school? Is touring an option?

And I know that there is going to be nothing happening with Rain City Talent. *Still* in high school? Suddenly I'm panicking again because *oh no*, last night was my chance, maybe my only chance ever to be free, and I blew it.

That's how I feel all the way to school. And then all day it's like the world is at a distance, everything bouncing off me, like I'm a metal shell of a person. Teachers like Ms. Rosaz and Mr. Travis tell Keenan and me **Good Job** like we have passed some kind of test, though they say it with serious faces, because they know what almost happened. I wonder if they're congratulating me because they think I decided at the last minute not to sing my lyrics. Which I did. But I still thought they'd be sung . . . I don't bother trying to explain that to them.

We walk by Ms. Tiernan in the hall between periods and she looks at me with a half smile and a nod and says, "Nicely done last night, boys."

I don't reply or show anything on my face, and then when we are a few steps away, enough that she won't hear, I open my mouth . . . but I don't curse under my breath like I was thinking I should. I just let her think she won, or whatever she thinks or whatever it is. I don't know.

Probably the first sign that things are basically over with Skye happens when I get to my locker in the morning. Keenan is there with his back-to-shaggy hair and for Skye the extra level of makeup is gone—because honestly, who can keep up the effort?—and the second I arrive she slams her locker shut and walks off with Meron and Katie.

But then at lunch Keenan and I are still stupid enough to sit with them like things are the same today as they were yesterday, and while I eat a bean salad and smell Keenan's cheeseburger and Tater Tots, the three of them huddle together and build an ice wall between us.

I don't have the energy to say anything. Finally Keenan asks, "What's up?"

"What do you *think* is up?" Skye snaps. "We both totally got in huge trouble with our parents last night for standing up and screaming the f-word at the concert because *somebody* betrayed us and decided to *sell out*!"

I look at her and I want to shout, *This was your plan! Your big idea! Why don't you care about what I went through, and what about all that stuff you said about how you believed in the song?!*

But I don't. It would all just come out like a mess and Skye's probably been stewing about it all night so she'll be ready with all these head-spinning reasons and arguments like ninja knives coming at me.

"Now," Skye says to her friends, "we need a location for the Winky rally. . . ." She's doing the talking-loud thing. I guess so that we can tell how not-part-of-their-plans we are. Whatever.

The worst part is that I sit there wondering if Skye is right. I know she was counting on me. How many other kids were too? And that makes it sound like I had some kind of responsibility to them. Did I?

Maybe I did sell out. But I don't think that's what I was thinking about up onstage. I wanted to sing the words, it was my chance, but then I could barely even play the chords and it was all zombie Hitler and it was too much because there was Ms. Tiernan, suspension, the end of the Rusty Soles, how Valerie felt, the whole crowd. . . .

When you add it all up, it's funny because it's almost like the song that was supposed to free us had become a trap. And so instead of the words being the escape, maybe up there on-stage, I was trying to escape the words. . . .

And I feel mad at Skye again because she grabbed my idea and totally took it where she wanted.

But it's not her fault I went along with it.

Just like it's not Keenan's fault he put up the song online and I didn't take it down. I let those things happen because they were so cool. I let everybody have a piece of me. And then I couldn't come through.

Maybe I wasn't ready to be the rock star.

Or maybe I didn't totally want to sing the words.

Sure, at the time, it bothered me thinking about changing them, but really, would it have been the end of the world? Except then it all became the end of the world. I can't let that happen next time, if there is a next time.

And I'm not going to say any of this to Skye. Instead, I stand up. "Come on," I say to Keenan.

He looks at me and for a second I don't know if he'll come with me. He could stay with the girls. I failed him. . . .

But he gets up without a word and we move to another table by ourselves.

Permanent Promotion

Free period is shortened because of the early dismissal for Thanksgiving break, so Keenan and I head straight for the student lounge. We find Mr. Darren sitting by the Marshall, testing instrument cables. He connects one, strums a little, then pulls it out and tries the next.

"Gentlemen," he says, smiling.

"Hey," I say.

"So how are you guys doing today?"

"Fine," says Keenan. He doesn't sound fine. On top of last night, I know he's super-disappointed about the Rain City Talent thing. Maybe about Meron too. I wonder if he blames me.

Then Mr. Darren says, "Hey, so I've gotten a lot of compliments on your performance last night."

"Yeah right," I say.

"It was pretty good." We look over to see Sadie on the couch, writing in her notebook. "I was there."

"It was rough," I say.

Now Sadie smiles. "Not bad for a rookie, though."

Normally I would not be okay with a seventh grader saying that, but then, Sadie knows. She's been up there in the blue light, done that thing that I tried to do. Well, close enough. "Thanks," I say. "So are you kicked out of this?"

"Nah," she says. "On probation. But I'll be back for winter quarter."

"Oh," I say, then manage to add, "cool." And so ends my lead singing career. Last night really was it. . . .

"Actually," says Mr. Darren, "I was just telling Sadie that it's probably best for everyone if she concentrates on the Random Sample for Spring Arts Night, since the Rusty Soles have a capable singer now."

Sadie stands and throws her bag over her shoulder. "Thanks for stealing my job." I wonder if she's mad but she smiles. "Being in two bands was such a burden." She says it like she did us some kind of huge favor and walks out.

"How does that sound?" says Mr. Darren.

"Good, I mean, maybe, yeah?" I say, and I turn to Keenan because I want to know if he's cool with it.

He flashes a glance at me, and there's the first smile I've seen all day. It's not a big one, but still. "Cool."

"So," says Mr. Darren, "about last night . . ." He checks a cable by hitting a huge G chord. My nerves rumble as I wonder what he'll say. "I know you were struggling with whether to sing your real lyrics. It looked like it ate you up a bit on-stage."

"Yeah," I say.

He sighs. "I'm not going to tell you that I think you made the right call, or anything like that. What I am going to say is that I'm glad that you're not suspended and kicked out of Rock Band. I don't think that would have been worth it."

I want to agree. I want to disagree too.

I just stand there.

"The important thing is to let last night be last night. It happened. Learn from it and let it go. The great thing about music is that there's always another gig."

Mr. Darren adds, "It's not like you're a figure skater and once you turn twenty you're too old or something. Okay, that was a weird reference, but my daughter, Camille, is totally obsessed with figure skating right now. My point is that you're going to get a lot more chances, and that's what matters, at least so says this over-the-hill rocker. You wrote a good song, and I'm excited because it was only your first."

"Okay," I say. It kinda sounds like grown-up-speak, but it also makes sense. There will be Spring Arts Night, and because of how last night worked out, we will actually get to play it. And we can definitely do way better next time.

I realize that what Mr. Darren has, as a has-been, is experience. He's been to the places I haven't been yet. I have a little more experience now too. But only a little.

"Speaking of which," says Mr. Darren, "we only have four months till showtime, so next week we should get cracking on the Rusty Soles' second big international hit. It will be our last show before you're off to high school stardom, so I want it to be amazing. Sound like a plan?"

"Yeah," I say. That sounds just fine.

"Totally," says Keenan.

"Good," says Mr. Darren. "And next week I want to show you some major seventh chords. Triumphant yet tragic, all at the same time. You'll love 'em." He checks another cable and strums a chord that is maybe going to be one of these mysterious major sevenths but the cable is bum and so there is just a little tinny sound of his fingers on strings.

I feel like there's something I want to say to Mr. Darren. I don't know exactly what it is. We stand there for a second and then I finally say, "Thanks, Mr. Darren."

He looks at us and smiles. "Rock and roll," he says, and starts swapping in the next cable.

In the Margins

The last period before Thanksgiving break is English. Luckily it's shortened too.

Ms. Rosaz hands back my notebook with the definitive list. "Anthony, that was the strongest work you've done this year. I hope I see more of it."

"Thanks," I mutter when she's not looking. I go to slide my notebook away, but then open up to the list. She's written a bunch of comments in the margin, like Clara always gets. One says: *This scene is so vivid. You transported me!* Another: *Very wise observation.* And by the Lamborghini she drew a smiley face.

I look around, kind of embarrassed. Then I read the comments again. Transported. Observation. Smiley face. These are all new for my notebook.

At the bottom she gave me 4/5 points (–1 because it was late) and wrote: *I hope you share more about your music!*

I close the notebook and think: *Maybe.*

The New Future

After school, Keenan and I start to walk home and it's one of those completely random days that can happen any time in Seattle: the clouds break up, the sun appears, and the temperature jumps to like sixty and it feels like summer even though it's practically winter.

The sun, and the fact that Skye and Meron and Katie are walking up ahead of us and doing their annoying three-headed-hydra thing—whispering and then all looking at us and then whispering again and busting out laughing—makes Keenan and me decide to just stop and grab a seat on the jungle gym until they're out of sight.

We climb up on the parallel bars and hang our feet down and we are like leopards sitting up lording over the little scrubby gazelles that look at us fearfully and stay away.

"They're so dumb," Keenan says, watching Skye, Katie, and Meron leave.

"Yeah," I agree.

"I didn't really like Meron anyway," he adds.

"Nah."

Then neither of us talks for a while.

Finally I say, "Almost four thousand plays this morning."

"Yeah," says Keenan.

I tilt my head to the sun. "It will be cool to write a new song," I say, "like Mr. Darren said."

Keenan is quiet for a second. I wonder if after last night he's sick of me and done with our dreams about all the band stuff or what, but then he says, "If we wrote three more songs, then we could make an EP. Hey, maybe we can scrape our money together and get seven-inches made."

"Ooh, let's get the red vinyl that's kinda see-through," I say.

"And we could do our own artwork and sell them over at Sonic Boom."

"Yeah," I say. I like those ideas. Things with Keenan and me seem to be fine. I sort of want to ask him if he's mad, but I don't. Maybe we are just going to move on to the next thing like we used to.

"Hey, guys."

I look down, squinting through green sunlight blobs, and there is Valerie. She's ditched her black wool hoodie and has this cool lavender Sister's Secret T-shirt, the one with the two hands cupped like they're hiding something. There's no one with her.

"Hey," I say. "You like Sister's Secret?"

"Nah." She smiles and I get that she's joking. "How are you?"

"Fine," I say, and I kinda do feel fine, for the first time all day.

Some little kids run by screeching. One bumps into Valerie's hip.

"Hey, *watch* it!" I bark at them, and it's funny to see them get so scared to death that one of the little freaks trips and falls and gets a face burn on the blue rubber playground surface but then doesn't want to cry in front of us and runs off. I'm about to laugh at that but then I see that Valerie is looking after the kid all concerned so I hold it in.

"I thought we played really well last night," she says. "It was probably tough for you."

I shrug. "I guess."

"Still," she says, "my dad was saying how tight we sounded. He plays bass so he kinda knows. He said you had a good tone, Keenan."

This makes Keenan sit up. "Cool," he says.

"And he said you had a unique voice, Anthony."

"Unique?" I say. "You mean like crappy and screwing up the words and stuff?"

Valerie rolls her eyes at me but also smiles. "It was only our first show," she says.

"Yeah," I agree, and I like the sound of that. I think I will be using that phrase, "only our first show," a lot in the next couple weeks.

And what Valerie just said is kinda like what Mr. Darren said, because it means there will be more chances. Last night wasn't the only one. Well, it was the only chance at *that* show. But if the next show could be awesome, then who would even remember last night? And if the one after that was even better, and so on . . .

And maybe that's sorta how it works, all of it, step by step, show by show, Fat Class by Fat Class, flax muffin by flax muffin . . . like mastering a level of *LF*, but more. Like maybe all of these campaigns in my life are long, and I am in these bands of brothers and we fight, level by level, slowly getting there.

Maybe it didn't all need to happen last night.

"You guys rocked," I say to Valerie and Keenan again. Even though I told them already, I want them to know how great they were, and in spite of everything this whole stupid week, they still got up on that stage and nailed it. Better than me. Better than everyone else. They were rock stars. Maybe that's why the crowd still applauded. I made it all about me. But what the audience saw was a band.

"Thanks," says Valerie. Then her face scrunches. "Hey, so, you guys like the Zombie Janitors, right?"

"They rock," I say.

"I heard you guys saying that you'd been learning songs from *Arcane Sweater Vest*," says Valerie, "so I checked it out. The beats are great."

"I know, right?" I say, and for the first time in what feels like forever I have that feeling like, how cool is it to hear a girl say that? And I realize that what I feel around Valerie, and what made it hard to feel like she didn't like my song or the choice about the lyrics, is *respect*.

Now she puts her hands half in her jean pockets but then pulls them right out again. "So, well, I was thinking, I've been learning them too, and I have a drum set at my house now. My parents said it would be cool if maybe you guys wanted to come over sometime, like to play some ZJ tunes."

"Nice," says Keenan. "Like a real band practice."

"Yeah," says Valerie. "I mean, that too. Because there's Rock Band, but there's only one more show for that, and then . . . well, if the Rusty Soles are going to start playing at the Vera Project and stuff next year, then we're going to need more than just two songs. Also, my dad knows the guy who books the summer shows over at Alki, like on the beach? That could rock . . . and then . . . Oh." Valerie stops and looks up almost like she just got caught. "Well, what do you guys think?"

What do I think? What I think is that I know now that Valerie has the dream too. The Rusty Soles playing Vera, or a beach party? That would be insane!

And I hadn't thought about this before, but really what she's talking about is actually only like six months away. By then, everything that we went up against last night will be long gone. No more caring about whether the words are appropriate or anything. And for the first time all year, the rest of eighth grade doesn't sound like forever. In fact, it's barely enough time to get a set together, an EP . . .

But then I remember that seconds are ticking by and Valerie needs an answer: "Definitely."

"Yeah," says Keenan.

But then I have another thought that just pops out. "But I thought you didn't like my song." I kinda feel like an idiot for saying it, but I can't help it.

Valerie blows at her bangs. "Well, just the end, but I listened to it some more and . . ." She shrugs. "It's very . . . you."

"Thanks," I say. "I might change the words anyway. Who knows?"

Valerie smiles. "Either way. But, um, do you think every song you write is going to have f-bombs in it?"

"I don't think so."

"Okay," she says, and I'm waiting for her to add "good" or something but she doesn't and actually I really like how with Valerie there's this extra level of figuring out between what she says and what she means, like her opinions aren't all *right there* in your face all the time like *some* people I know. I have to think about what she's saying.

"So," she goes on, "are you guys around after Thanksgiving? Maybe we could practice Saturday or Sunday?"

"Yeah," I say. Keenan agrees.

She smiles and her face squints double in the sun. "Great. We'll set it up online. Well, see ya later." She makes a little wave and starts to walk away.

"Later," I call after her.

Keenan and I leave soon too. We head for the comics shop, walking slow in the sun, and I am thinking about Valerie, and about what she said, and how we'll need more songs. For practice, shows, EPs, New York, all of it.

Some of these songs might be like "Breakout," because we are not out of the trenches yet, but I also want to write some songs that feel like today. More sunny. . . . A song that Valerie would think is cool.

The War Rages On

The final movie scene at the end of *Liberation Force 4.5* shows you and your band of brothers celebrating in the streets of Paris, partying all night.

But then bright and early the next morning your commanding officer kicks you out of bed and gives you new orders. You're being shipped out to the Pacific, departing immediately. You turn to your mates and nod grimly, and then text appears announcing the sequel coming out next summer: *Liberation Force 5.0: Island Honor*. And you feel psyched because now you know that the battle continues. The war isn't over. It's on to the next campaign.

There will be more chances to rock.

I can't wait.

A NOTE FROM THE AUTHOR

Spend enough time around kids and teens, and their voices start to get in your head. I met the teens who inspired *Breakout* while teaching creative writing classes at a K–8 public school in Seattle, through a program called Writers in the Schools.

Anthony is based on a particular type of eighth grader I taught each year: low-achieving, regularly disruptive in class, and often acting disinterested. Whether he actually is disinterested or not, he doesn't know how to express himself positively, and may not have been recognized when he tried. It's a lot safer to fit in by acting out.

One afternoon, I stopped by the after-school rock band club and saw two boys and a girl that I'd struggled with in class absolutely rocking out. They seemed talented and sure of themselves, and so enthusiastic. Afterward, I tried to get them to write about this experience in the classroom to mixed results, but at least we could connect as musicians.

When I started hearing Anthony's voice in my head and writing this story, I realized how much empathy I had for teens in this moment. Anthony doesn't want to be a bad kid. But how else is he going to break out of the trap he's in? I also wanted to present Anthony with the essential challenge of any artist trying to find their voice: when you finally get the stage, what do you want to say?

There's a reason swears exist in our language. I remember using them as far back as elementary school. After fifteen years in classrooms, it seems to me that while of course it makes sense to have rules about language and conduct, it's also important to talk about the meaning and impact of *every* word, including profanity. I didn't set out to write a novel about the f-word, though this manuscript was at one point titled *One Little Word* and briefly *The F-Word*. In the end, those titles seemed to sell Anthony's predicament short. That said, I do hope that this book can serve as an opportunity for discussion about what words are capable of, whether we're eighth graders, or former eighth graders.

It took many years to get this manuscript right, and to find an editor and publisher who were willing to champion it. I'm so grateful to Phoebe Yeh for sticking her neck out for this book, and for helping me shape it into something better than I'd ever imagined. Also thanks to everyone at Crown and Random House for getting behind it. I'm indebted, as always, to George Nicholson and the team at Sterling Lord Literistic for believing in this story throughout its journey. Thank you to my readers, who remind me why I do this. And I continue to be grateful to the teachers, librarians, and booksellers who support my work, and to my fellow authors, friends, and family for their love and understanding.

Allied V for Victory,
Kevin